Praise (sort of) for "Happy Holidays!"

"a vibrant and good natured narrative…a joy to read"
  - Launchpad Prose Competition (Finalist)

"fast-paced and hilarious…a highly enriching reading experience"
  - Pikasho Deka for Readers' Favorite

"Charlie Barnes is one of those characters that you just can't help cheering for, even though you kinda know you shouldn't. Highly Recommend."
  - Stevie G, UK Amazon Reviewer

"I was laughing out loud more times than I can remember. This is a perfect light vacation read."
  - critical.dk, US Amazon Reviewer

"This isn't really so much of a romance, but still a good read."
  - Kjnrose, US Amazon Reviewer

"As God is my witness, the events in Chapter 5 did not happen! I would never wear white in November."
  - Desiree Adalicia Masters

"There's no sex! Why isn't there any sex? It's a gay comedy, there should be sex, and lots of it!"
  - Andrew's Mom

Happy Holidays!

HAPPY HOLIDAYS!

How I Went from Failed Writer to Drug Mule, and Back, Without Really Trying

The Charlie Barnes Experience
Vol. 1

C.R. "Charlie" Barnes

Beach Book Press

For S.
He's not mean,
he's just self-focused.

A Note from the Author

Yes, I know, I've heard it a million times if I've heard it once, "This isn't *really* a *'holiday book'* it just happens during the Holidays." And of course, everyone who says that is right. So what? Read to the end and you'll understand. But, also, can't we have a 'holiday book' without all the trappings and trimmings? Do we need jingly bells and snowmen? I mean, we can have romance books without sex, can't we? I think we can. Now that we have that out of the way, I hope you enjoy my little book. It was a blast to write and it still makes me laugh when I read it to myself, which I often do because I haven't written the next book yet because something about pandemics and politics and wars, and all the realness of reality has crushed my sense of humor.

But I'm working on it, believe you me, I am. I'm single-handedly keeping Grey Goose in business. I just…I don't know…the second book is called "Adulting" and, well, where's the fun in that? They tell me it's there, if you look hard enough. But dang, it seems like a lot of work. It really is a minor miracle *this* book was finished. Hey, there it is, a miracle! That's Holiday-ish, isn't it? Holiday adjacent, maybe? I'm going with it. The point is, however you feel about holidays and books, this one is meant to be fun, so enjoy it already. Oh, and fair warning, there's no graphic sex. Sex does happen, what would *life* be without it? But no, there are no details. You'll have to use your imagination. Or wait for the movie. Probably better if you go with the first option.

CHAPTER ONE

Recognition

"Dorothy, wake up," Smack, Smack, these words and two gentle slaps on my face, "Come on now, show me some life." The first thing I recognize as I come to. Blood is oozing from various parts of my face. Second recognition - the hand slapping me belongs to a cop. Standing over me, gorgeous, even through a swollen eye.

Lying in the street. Not the street exactly. A parking lot, but I'm close to the street. Which means every asshole in a car gets to drive by and laugh. My third recognition. How lovely. It's raining again, more like misting. A mist is enough.

I'm lying there, wet, bloody, wearing a powder-blue gingham dress, ruby red slippers and bows in my hair. I have a stuffed dog Velcro'd to my side... or I did. Getting the picture?

Flash... memory of a fist driving hard into my face. Flash... next memory of a boot slamming into my ribs... the ones I broke last May. One last flash, and crunch, as the same boot crushes the bridge of my nose... the source of all this blood pouring out onto everything. Thank God I finally blacked out. Ever tried to fight on wet pavement in size 13 patent leather Mary Janes? Tricky.

Here's this cop… this beautiful strapping paragon of manhood… standing over me. Slapping me, saying, as a southern cop says, "Wake up Door – Ahh – theee," smack, smack.

Love at first blurred sight.

"Auntie em… Auntie em…," I sigh as I look… or try to look… into his big ice-blue cop's eyes. Hell no, I'm not dropping out of character. He sees I'm back and I see a smile splash across his face.

It's a struggle to stand up… he helps. My dress is a mess, twisted you might say. My hero helps me get the damn thing back in place, covering my bits and bobbles. Miracles all around.

He speaks again, still smiling, "Looks like the Wicked Witch had her way with you." How nice, a sense of humor.

"You should see the other bitch." Blood and flecks of… something… spray into the air. He steps back, the smile vanishes.

"Sorry," I spray again and start to wobble on my feet.

He reaches out, the hero once more, "Sit down and wait for the ambulance, it'll be here any minute."

"Ambulance? I don't need no stinkin' ambulance." Trying to sound butch, but wearing a dress. Damnit. What a cliché, wear a dress for Halloween and I'm about to be carted off to the hospital. No way, not this cowboy.

"Look…" he starts.

Then an interruption.

"Uh-uh, honey, you may be fine to look at but you are not takin' my Dorothy off in an ambulance like some piece of meat."

At last, it's my Good Witch Glinda, (aka BeeBee), come to save me. Where the hell was he five minutes ago?

Here he comes, not walking, striding, through the parking

lot. The crowd of gawkers parts like the sea before Moses, his white gown, yes, he made it himself, and yes calling it a dress is a crime, his white gown flowing behind him and a fabulous headdress looking more like a weapon every minute. This is not his first adventure in drag.

"Honey you are not taking my Dorothy away like a pack of flying monkeys. You call them people back and tell 'em you don't need what they're sellin'."

He's fallen back on his accent, waving his hand, he's a sight to behold and hear. BeeBee is six foot-six, with the body of a marble statue, and the attitude of a Mother Superior. When he gets worked up, you best watch yourself.

Born on St. Thomas to a white businessman father and Caribbean night club singer, he managed to inherit the best of both parents, with most of the best coming from his mother.

He's fierce, even out of drag. But tonight, he's taken it up a few notches. White sequined gown, most of the front removed to reveal washboard abs, and pecks to make a girl jealous. Cocoa-butter-creamy-smooth skin, and of course there's the package. Tonight, there's nothing at all discreet about this outfit. The package is truly awe inspiring.

The four foot stilts he's walking on only serve to enhance the effect.

Back to the cop. He looks The Good Witch up and down, nice and slow. Then he looks at me, and before he can speak, I tell him, blood and snot flowing freely, "This is Glinda.... Glinda, say hello to my future husband."

Squinting at his name tag, he seems embarrassed, exactly what I wanted. His name is Goode. Officer Goode. "I'm the future Missus Goode," I say, gesturing for them to come together. Glinda extends a hand, as if waiting for a bow and a kiss.

Officer Goode ain't buyin' it.

He smiles and says, "Hello," then to me, "you need to get

to the hospital."

He's concerned. I'm in love.

"No," Glinda says curtly.

"But Glinda, all this blood…my dress, it's ruined."

"Bitch, this is Halloween, do you understand, Hall-ohh-weeeeeen. This is our night. Don't let this shit get in the way. We'll tell everybody this is your costume. You might even win a contest. We'll call you 'Little Red Riding Hood with Her Ass Kicked.' The blood adds some color to your pasty face for a change."

"I don't have a hood," I protest. I think I might rather spend more time with My-Hero-Officer-Goode.

"Uh-uh Dorothy…we're takin' over the Emerald City tonight. We'll get you cleaned up and we'll be back in the game, come on bitch, get your Toto and let's get shakin'."

Officer Goode intervenes, "Wait a minute, I have to fill out a report, I've got questions."

Glinda interrupts, "Questions? What the hell have you been doin' out here? Questions? Don't you know what happened? Hate crime!"

Officer Goode is offended. Something approximating speech passes from my brain to my lips, "Glinda, dear, don't swear at the nice policeman, please."

She snaps a look at me, a quick flash of a smile. A hint of recognition, under those vicious eyes, "Uhhh-huh," is all she utters.

"Not a hate crime," and it's true. "Not at all."

Officer Goode takes out a notebook and pen, positions his pen over the paper, and looks at me expectantly. His eyes are undeniable. Or is it irresistible? Who cares, they're pretty.

My story is interrupted by Glinda before it begins, "Fine, Dorothy, you do what you want, you always do, it's why you're in this mess. You can get on without Glinda."

Glinda makes a dramatic swooshing pirouette on her stilts

and prances back to the party.

Officer Goode, my Hero, smiles again. Alone together at last.

I begin to tell him how a nice guy like me ended up in a dress like this. "It was my fault. If you want the full story, it's gonna take…"

He smiles and interrupts, "Do you want to press charges?"

"No," I spray. The more I talk, the more my lip bleeds. Thankfully he's out of range.

"Why not? If they did this to you, they could do it to someone else."

I try to laugh, but my ribs respond with a hard 'no.' What comes out sounds more like a choke. I gag, he steps back some more. Damn, I gotta fix this again.

"No, they won't. I'm sure this was a one off."

"You know him?"

He's got me. "Know? In what sense?"

He's annoyed. The situation is rapidly worsening.

"Okay, okay, yes, I know him. I caused this. No, I deserved it." It's not entirely a lie. I don't know the guy, but I know who sent him and why.

Officer Goode's face melts like butter on a hot biscuit, "Nobody deserves this… I can't keep calling you Dorothy. Let's start with your name."

Ship is getting back on course. We hear the siren, my chariot approaches. Time is of the essence.

The world starts spinning, my ability to remain upright becomes uncertain. "Sure, sure…" oozes out of me. Sounds more like, "shursh, shursh." My lip is absurdly fat. I can't see out of one eye. I'm wheezing because my ribs are crushed. What a picture. Awesome.

"Charlie Barnes." Which sounds more like "Sharwee pawns." Speech is no longer one of my core skills, it's not clear if he understands.

The ambulance pulls into the parking lot. My audience dissipates, but new arrivals start to fill the ranks. Moths to the flames of the flashing reds and whites.

"OK Charlie, the cavalry is here. How about a phone number and address?"

He must be joking because, why not? I reach inside my bra. Yes, I have fake tits. My Dorothy isn't flat-chested. Not sixteen either, but nobody's perfect.

My non-blood-drenched hand locates the card and presents it to him.

The EMTs approach and ask me to kindly have a seat in their fancy ride. My feet try to trip each other and a nice beefy lesbian helps me walk. I do love strong women.

The lights start to dim, every sound seems like it's coming from miles away, there's an echo in my ears and my last coherent thought is, "Oh shit, I'm passing out again."

My face plants itself squarely between Beefy Lesbian EMT's breasts, and somewhere far, far away I hear a member of my audience shout, "There's no place like home Dorothy, you...."

And I'm gone. More precisely, everything is gone, total nothingness.

Then I'm coming back.

"Skank? Dorothy's not a skank...why would someone call Dorothy a skank?" I mumble to no one. Of all the things I could say upon waking up in the ER. My life gets better by the minute.

Wait, not the ER. More complicated, less crowded. The ICU? This isn't my dress. What is this? How is it daylight? Future Husband was right, I don't deserve this. And yet.

Apparently having a heartbeat gets attention in the ICU. A nice nurse-looking lady approaches.

"Welcome back," says the cheery nurse lady.

"There's no place like home," I instantly regret saying.

"How are we doing today, Dorothy?"

We? Why is she happy? "Do you have my ruby red slippers? Where's Toto?" I can't help myself.

A normal person would ask something like, "Where am I? How long have I been here? Is this heaven or hell?" You know, normal. She laughs hard enough to work her Adam's apple into a frenzy. Wait a minute. She notices the utter what-the-hell-is-happening-here look on my face. She handles it like a pro.

"You're not the only one who likes blue gingham dresses, sweet cheeks." Then she starts doing all her nurse-work, checking things, measuring things, all the nurse stuff they can do while carrying on a conversation. Of course she's seen me naked. I do have sweet cheeks, not to be boastful, but I do. Good to know they're appreciated even here, where cheeks abound. Has anyone in the history of hospitals ever gotten one of those gowns properly closed? I think not.

"I'll take it as a compliment." My speech is nearly perfect, my fat lip is no longer corpulent. Seems I've been here a while. Time for some adulting, real questions on their way.

"What's your name?"

"You can call me Gale. Nurse Gale."

You have got to be shitting me. "Are we related?" Because normal questions are on pause.

"Aren't you clever. Most guys who do Dorothy never bother with her last name. How adorable."

Her upbeat attitude makes me feel like I should vomit, or something, to bring her back down to earth. But no, it would be worse for me, let's not.

"You have been one popular patient. A lawyer, a publisher, a policeman. Tell me Mister Barnes, are all your friends pretty?"

Policeman? My full attention has arrived. "Please. Call me Charlie. Did you happen to get the officer's name?"

"Of course we did. ICU visits are restricted. He claims you proposed to him in the Xanadu parking lot. How romantic Mister Barnes."

I see her. She's not cheery, she's a snarky bitch. We're getting somewhere. This is workable. "Please. Charlie. When was he here?"

She seems to be finished with her nurse duties, leaving…

"Not my day to manage your calendar Mister Barnes," she tosses over her shoulder like spilled salt.

Damn, wait, at least one proper question. Sitting up, pain, stupid me. My ribs scream, "hell no."

"Wait, come back," I wheeze.

For a moment she's gone. My body becomes a sack of potatoes, falls back, eyes to the ceiling. Then the quack-quack of her horrible rubber shoes as she returns. Shoes worthy of hatred, but in this context, I'll make them my ally, a secret spy. She'll never sneak up on me again.

"Mr. Barnes you need to be careful. You're not out of the forest yet. What can I do for you?"

Forest? It's 'woods.' Everyone knows the saying is out of the woods. Oh, I get it, I'm still Dorothy to her. Fine, I'm in a forest. Albeit not an enchanted one.

Mister Barnes again. Screw it, she can call me Father Christmas if she wants. My surrender is unconditional.

"How long have I been here?"

She has a syringe. She's putting something in my IV.

"Something for the pain." She finishes drugging me, puts the syringe in a red box stuck on the wall. She looks directly into my eyes, which means she's leaning over the bed, looking down on me. A baby in a cradle.

Here it comes.

"Mr. Barnes, this may be a bit of shock. This is day five of your visit to the Intensive Care Unit of the luxurious Grady Memorial Hospital."

Five days. Five missing days. And then, like bombs, snippets of memory begin exploding in my brain. My presence has been less than pleasant for the ICU staff. I have been a problem child. I take my best shot.

"I'm sorry."

Then it happens. She smiles a genuine, sweet, kind, smile. She rests her hand on my shoulder, Nurse Nightingale, at last.

"It's OK Charlie. Shit happens. You're not the worst patient we've had, not by a long measure. Get some rest. The doctor will be in to see you soon."

Then she's gone. A lovely warm comfy sensation sweeps across my body. Could have been her, could have been the drugs. Who knows? Who cares? It's been a hard day, time for a nap.

CHAPTER TWO

Good News, Bad News

What the hell is wrong with doctors and nurses? Why do they always have to wake you up to do whatever it is they want to do? I'm sleeping, come back later.

To call me cranky would be to underestimate my feelings.

It would be better if the doctor was a handsome young man, but no, she's reasonably good-looking woman in her forties with a total "I'm in charge here and you're my work product, shut up and do as I say" attitude. She's mean. I like her.

"Mr. Barnes, you still with me?"

Of course not. "I'm having trouble focusing. Still groggy." All she's got is bad news. "Please, call me Charlie. I hate being called Mister Barnes." This is the truth, which finds its way to me from time to time.

"Fine, Charlie. Please try to focus. I have other patients…"

Really? This isn't all for me? How disappointing.

"…who need me more than you. You're on the mend…"

At last, good news.

"…you'll be transferred out of the ICU sometime later tonight."

"Why not right away?" Reverse psychology. There's no rush. Nurse Gale makes me feel special, as do the pain meds.

"It's a process, it takes time. We'll get to you as soon as we can. Do you have any other questions?"

Strictly business. Two can play this game. "Yes, pain management, what's the plan?" See? Business.

"I'll write for acetaminophen with codeine for the next two days. Once you're discharged, you should do fine with any non-prescription pain reliever."

"Doesn't sound like much fun." Again, honesty. She gets the joke. We'll be besties in no time.

"You'll be fine Mister Barnes. Good luck to you." She leaves. Yet another woman walks out of my life. Better off.

Like a vision sent down from on high, through my open door I see My Hero Officer Goode stepping off an elevator. BeeBee is with him. I think to myself, "Self, why are they together?"

Hmmm… they greet the doctor, she looks over her shoulder at me and smiles. The door closes, end scene. Why was she smiling? What are they up to? It's a conspiracy, I'm sure of it. They're all laughing. Yep, definitely something there. When they finish their small talk and come to my room, BeeBee comes through the door first.

"Charlie, you've come back to us, resurrected. We missed you." He momentarily commands the attention of everyone in the ICU. He sweeps over me like a gentle tide on a low beech, kisses me on the forehead and gently strokes my cheek.

The door closes, Officer Goode arrives at my bedside and takes my hand, what, no kiss? Geez. Then he crushes my heart. "You gave us a real scare Charlie. Glad to see you looking better."

"Who is us?"

He looks at BeeBee and says, "Brian and I have been

getting to know each other. He's told me a lot about you."

Fuck you BeeBee, what have you done? I don't say it. And how does he know your name already? Instead, I give BeeBee a look. He reads it perfectly.

"Don't you get all hot and bothered. Luke and I have been worried sick about you."

The hurt seems real. Wait. Luke?

"Your name is Luke? Luke Goode? As in, you sure Luke Goode to me?" No wonder he's a cop, his parents plastered a 'kick my ass' sign to his back at birth.

"Gee Charlie, good joke, never heard it before," he says with more than a hint of sarcasm. He lets go of my hand, and I am ruined.

"Well, I'm here all week. Be sure to tip your servers and bartenders."

His perfect nose on his perfect face gives me a burning desire to look in a mirror.

"How's my face? Please be honest."

BeeBee answers first with, "You look like somebody crossed a potato with an eggplant, and stuck a wig on it."

Luke's "It's not too bad" doesn't help.

For a moment, a brief moment, crying becomes an option. It's obvious because BeeBee drops his accent and shifts into his lawyer persona. In other words, he gets real.

"Charlie, I'm not gonna lie. You look like shit. But you'll get better. Plastic surgery will get your nose sorted out. The scar on your lip, it could be sexy, you never know. But here's the thing, you had a nasty concussion, and you survived. You're getting out of here in a couple of days and you'll get back to normal in no time. Dez says this might help your sales. And, the best part for you, Luke isn't the least put off by your eggplant-potato face."

He's got at least one good point in his speech. My turn to be sarcastic, "Thanks BeeBee, helpful." I'm vain. I liked my nose the way it was. Probably shouldn't have gotten it kicked in.

"I need some coffee. Nurse Gale showed me where they make the good stuff. Luke, want a cup?"

"Yes, thank you," he says, sweet like a sugar cookie.

BeeBee leans down, as if for another quick kiss, but no. He whispers in my ear.

"You've got 10 minutes, don't screw this up."

BeeBee stands, spins, flings the door open and strides into the heart of the ICU like he owns the place. For a moment it's awkward. Luke takes my hand again, smiling at me. No idea what BeeBee's told him, but he's here, it can't all be bad. Or does he like bad? Let's kick this off.

"No uniform today?" It's a start.

"I'm off today. But you won't see me in one again. I was promoted, you can call me Detective Goode, or Luke, take your pick."

He says this as one might say, 'I'll have a number one with a Coke.'

"Where to start, why you're here on your day off, or hey, congrats on the promotion. For the record, I liked the uniform. Tight in all the right places."

He laughs, releases my hand too fast for me to tighten my grip, and pulls a chair alongside the bed. He sits and is looking directly into my face, an act of bravery.

"I'm here because I wanted to see you, I don't want to talk about me."

"Should I be nervous, detective?" Half joking, half serious.

"I want to know what you remember about the assault, who did this to you, why. You said you knew the guy…"

"Anything else, because you're already asking a lot."

"Yes. I want a date. When you get out of the hospital, I want to cook dinner for you."

"Wow." Dammit, 'wow' as a first response, pathetic. Must

be lingering head-wound issues.

"Wow? You can't do better than wow?"

Is he reading my mind? "Are you reading my mind?"

Another sweet chuckle, then back to serious.

"I wish. But no, I have to settle for getting you to talk to me. It's tedious."

He gives me a minute to think. Sits there, sweet look of concern on his face, staring into my eggplant, waiting for me to answer. When was the last time I was serious about anything? This must be what BeeBee didn't want me to screw up.

"I'll tell you everything, with some conditions. First, it has to wait. I don't want to think about it today."

"Fine."

"Second, no fish. It's a date if we don't have fish."

"I'm not exactly a pescatarian. Anything else?"

"Yes, one more thing, you have to promise me you won't arrest anyone for this. It'll make things worse."

There's the rub, he has to promise not to do exactly what a cop, a detective, is supposed to do. This is the moment we find out if it's true love or a passing romance. Or something else entirely.

He leans back in his chair, takes a deep breath, and lets out a nice slow exhale. His breath is delicious, and it gives me second thoughts about the last condition. I want a date.

"Now who's asking for a lot?"

"I want this in the rearview as soon as possible. If you arrest them, it keeps this hanging around forever."

It's a big bucket of bullshit, but it's all I got.

He shakes his head, I'm expecting the 'no' any second. Brace yourself.

He looks me in the eyes again, places his hand on his heart, and speaks the words which will forever change the course of my life. I'm being melodramatic, but it's true.

"I promise you, Charlie Barnes, I, Detective Luke Goode, upon hearing your true confession, will not arrest anyone you mention for any act committed which placed you in this hospital bed."

Could he be more specific? What the hell? Screw it, it's a good deal, fair enough. I hold my hand out to him, curl my fingers under my thumb with my pinky finger extended. He looks puzzled.

"Pinky swear."

There's his smile. I heart his smile. I wanna do all manner of things with his smile.

He locks his pinky in mine and says, "Pinky swear."

The deal is done.

***

The next two days pass like a kidney stone, the lone bright point being the appearance of my publisher, Desiree.

Let's paint a picture of Desiree Adalicia Masters.

Whip-smart, mildly clever, has gobs of money. She's drop-dead gorgeous, if you like tall, slender women with perfect wavy drapes of strawberry blonde hair. She hates heavy makeup, what you see is what you get. She spends a fortune on her clothes, and it shows. She's my publisher, she's ruthless, and I love her like an old soul record.

Also, she has perfect breasts. They don't interest me, but some people care about such things. For those who do, there it is. Or they are. You get the point.

Desiree's family traces their lineage back to the Pilgrims, Mayflower Originals she calls them. It seems she's descended from some gal who saw the Salem Witch Trials first-hand and decided to take her chances in the forest with the wolves. Dez, as we of the inner circle call her. If you think you have a tough job, professional boxer, bull rider, crocodile wrangler, think again. A successful book publisher can take them all.

And Dez is the definition of success.

The one stain on her record is me.

To be fair, since it's me I'm talking about, my first book was a success. Naturally I wrote another one. If one book pays well, two should be even better, right? Not exactly. The dream died with the second bad review. And the third, and fourth, and you see where this is going.

Which brings me to my next book. Book three is overdue, like a long-forgotten library checkout, or a month-old open bottle of milk in a broken-down refrigerator. Haven't even started it.

Thankfully, Dez came bearing good news, although tempered by bad news. "Which do you want first?"

It's a loathsome question. Who cares if the egg came before the chicken or the chicken was birthed from a platypus. Give me the damn news, form the sentences and spit it out.

No, I did not speak those words to Dez. "Oh Dez, I trust you, use your best judgment."

I saw a movie once where one guy tells another he believes friendship is a measure of how much bullshit we're willing to buy from each other. I live by this definition. Except with Desiree Adalicia Masters. She doesn't buy bullshit from anybody. Not me, not her husband, not even her true best friend.

Which is why she responds to me with, "Sure. Good news first, then you can wallow in the bad."

Now you know why I love her.

"Your sales are through the roof. You're a star again. Happy? And, they don't have any photos."

Again? I've always been a star. Twinkle, twinkle. Photos? "I like this news. When do I get paid?"

"Time for the bad news."

"Give it to me," I say with my best who-gives-a-damn-about-bad-news inflection.

"We're holding back your royalties until you deliver on your next book, at least up to the amount of your advance."

"Don't we have a contract?" Of course she can do it, I read the contract. Or more precisely, BeeBee read it and gave me the highlights.

"Did you read it?"

What is going on? My skull gets cracked open and everyone can read my mind. This sucks.

"There's more."

Outstanding. "Let's hear it."

"Your sales are up because you've been all over the news. They're saying you're a victim of a hate crime. We think your new-found fans are sympathy buyers, not readers. Judging by the sales distribution across both books, I'd say they're right."

This leaves me speechless. Of course, she continues.

"It's not clear who spooled up the rumor mill, but, like I said, no one thought to take pictures of you in your Halloween costume. Or they did, but no one will publish them because it undermines their narrative."

Photos, got it.

My head hurts. This is not funny. Everything in my life is supposed to be funny, unless I don't want it to be funny. I want this to be funny. There's no way.

"Dez, this wasn't a hate crime and I'm not a victim. We have to get out in front of this."

"You think? Whatsoever shall we do? Who could we possibly call at a moment like this?"

Clever. The sarcasm was earned. She has a plan. She's enjoying the challenge. Hooray, I'm interesting again.

"We're issuing a statement, short and sweet." She presents me with a thin folder. "Read it, sign it, we'll get it out today."

I'm about to ask her a question as I open the folder, then I don't have to, there's a sticky note smack in the middle of the single page document, "Don't be an idiot, sign it. Love,

BeeBee."

"Do you have a pen?"

She makes her 'of course I do' face and hands me a pen.

"Did BeeBee help you write this?"

"No, we have people for such things as this, experts."

Experts who won't bill me. Let's add it to the list of good news for today.

"There's one more thing," she says, taking the folder from me.

I feel a trap closing. A mildly clever trap.

"We'll need your next book by the end of the month. No screwing around anymore Charlie, you need to put in the work."

I want to be strong. I want to say 'and if I don't' but I know her and I know me.

"I assume there are consequences if I fail to deliver."

"I'll personally rip up your contract, send you the shredded scraps, and put you out in the cold, looking for a new publisher. You'll need an agent this time around too. Imagine starting over at this point in your career, it might be fun for you."

"Apparently I'm hot these days."

She fails to appreciate the humor.

"Charlie, you're hot for all the wrong reasons. We're gonna put out the fire, today. It doesn't mean we can't capitalize on the situation. We'll get through a cooling off, you'll finish your book, and while we're moving it through the system, we can start promoting it. This is your chance to make lemonade."

Her favorite saying.

"Are you saying I'm a lemon?"

"No. I'm telling you to squeeze."

What a line, I could do a lot with it. However, despite what some people say, I'm not always a moron. It's time for contrition. Let's be clear though, I'm not contrite. "Thank you, Dez. I'll make it a priority as soon as I get home."

"You're not hearing me, Charlie. You get home, sit down at the handsome desk I gave you, put those fingers on the keys, and write the damn book. Make it your singular priority."

She's mad. Might as well keep poking the bear.

"You mean finish. Finish the damn book."

"Do you have pages for me?"

My bluff has been called. I was never good at poker.

I tap my head. "It's all up here"

"I don't want to cut you loose, but this is do or die. Understood?"

It couldn't be any clearer. Truth is, the book isn't written because, conceptually speaking, it sucks. It does. It's even worse than the last one. There's this great big epic in my head, and whatever I write down, it rips like a fart in an elevator. And I can't blame it on the guy standing next to me. Not this time.

"End of the month?"

"Yes," she hisses.

"What's today's date?"

"The seventh," she hisses again.

"Do I get a break for Thanksgiving?"

The bear has been thoroughly poked.

"Stop being a lazy little prick and do the work."

She left it there and walked out in a huff, which hurt more than you might think. Lazy is a fair assessment, and I can be a prick, but to string those words with 'little,' that's a special kind of mean. But the worst part? I'm being discharged.

She was my ride home.

CHAPTER THREE

Homecoming

My mailman hates me. Mail person. Mail woman. I don't know, I've never met them. However they identify, they hate me. How do I know? Because while I was in the hospital getting re-infamous, people started sending me mail, cards, letters, stuffed 'get well' animals, all sorts of crap. Amazing how fast it can build up in a few days.

The mailboxes in my building are small. It's not a fancy building. There's no doorman, no front desk, nothing. And it's old. There's a vestibule with retro-fitted punch-key access doors and tiny mailboxes with tiny brass doors.

True story about the boxes, our little community once had a raging debate over them. It went on for months. Modernize and upsize, versus accept and preserve. The Modernize hit squad eventually coerced enough votes out of the 'I don't give a shit crowd' to win the day. Then they started getting bids. Turns out, those snooty bitches are cheap as hell.

The wound may never heal.

It's late evening when I get home. I've never been as tired. There was the time I didn't sleep for forty-eight hours, but drug-induced insomnia doesn't count. It was a long time ago, let's forget I mentioned it.

I was tired.

Opening my brass box, I discover how much the potentially non-binary mail person hates me. A week's worth of mail is stuffed into the box. Every last piece of mail has been crushed and compacted. Those little stuffed animals? They don't exist, I made them up. There's no way I'm dealing with this. I shut the door. Problem solved.

It doesn't matter. BeeBee handles all my bills. He handles all my finances, and gives me an allowance.

I drag myself up the stairs. I'm on the fifth floor. No, there's no elevator. I love my building. It's one of two five story walk-ups, nestled into a midtown block (don't get excited, it's Atlanta, not Manhattan, I am not rich. Comfortable, yes. Rich, no.) near the corner of 10th and Peachtree. Like the title of a soap opera, my building is on Peachtree Place.

I can see Margaret Mitchell's house from my balcony.

She hated the house. Who can blame her? It wasn't even hers. She lived in an itty-bitty apartment, wrote at a teeny tiny desk, and took ten years to finish her single greatest work. She claimed she had the entire book in her head before she ever started writing, which doesn't ring true for me. If it is true, why'd it take ten years to write? My bet is she thought it sucked and kept putting it off. And it might suck, I've never read it. Not my cup of tea.

Poor Margaret. She hits a home run of a book, then war breaks out, then she gets killed by a drunk driver. She spent five days in the hospital before she died.

You see, Margie and I have a few things in common. We both take forever to write anything. We both had prolonged visits to Grady Hospital. And then there's the porn. Sorry, not porn. If you're a Pulitzer-winning novelist it's 'erotica.' If you're anyone else, it's plain old porn. She liked to read it, and might have tried to write it. Depends on who you talk to.

You can look all this up on the inter-webs.

The point is, other writers have taken their sweet-ass time to finish a book. She took ten years. Ten. Years.

I've got less than a month. And I got nothin'.

All of this is swirling around my head as I drag my sad sack up the stairs. All I want is to get inside, take a bath, make a drink, and watch anything my streaming service saved while I was laid up. Skipping commercials is the best. It's the little things in life.

Imagine my surprise, then, when arriving at my door I discover it's not locked. In fact, it's ajar. The lights are on and music is playing. Have I come to the wrong door? Not possible, there's one unit on the fifth floor, and it's mine. I smell something. It smells like… lasagna?

Has my Hero, Detective Luke, broken into my home, put on my favorite chill music (Diane Birch, for the record. But only her first album, which I got for free.), and cooked my favorite meal? Can it be?

No, it can't.

I open the door. It's a big place. When I bought it, I planned to rip out all the walls and open everything up, throw in modern appliances in a fancy 'chef's' kitchen, pile in some amazing furniture, and live the life.

Sidebar, what exactly is a chef's kitchen? Bullshit term. You heard it from me. Make note of it.

Instead of following through on my plans, I wrote my second book. I made some basic improvements and still have the furniture I moved in with. The new appliances are from a scratch-and-dent warehouse store in a happy town named Tucker. I like the name Tucker. Figure it out.

But I digress.

I open the door. It's warm, it smells fantastic, and "Fire Escape" is playing at the perfect volume. I kid you not, this is what I came home to.

I step into the living room, "BeeBee, I'm home." I know it's BeeBee. BeeBee knows me well enough to pull this off. BeeBee cares enough to try. BeeBee has a key. Then who should appear from the kitchen, wearing a ridiculous apron someone gave me for Christmas one year?

Someone who did not know me. It is, in fact, my hero Detective Luke Goode, and boy does he ever. He stands there, wearing an apron over a nice tight t-shirt, holding a pan of God's gift to humanity, lasagna, and he smiles and says, "Hello handsome. Welcome home."

Not a lie, not a dream, not a hallucination, he was there.

Exhausted, still bruised and battered, still foggy-brained, something happened. A switch got flipped, a knob got turned, use whatever terms you like. But right then and there I knew one thing with absolute certainty.

BeeBee talks too much.

Perhaps he'll get a thank you card someday. I close the door. I drop my plastic bag from the hospital containing my blue gingham dress, Toto (they found him), and all the plastic crap they sent me home with, and I soak it in for a few seconds. Then, because I'm an incurable romantic, I ask "How did you get in here?"

The best sign Luke and I might have a chance? He starts laughing. Not a mean laugh, or a chuckle, or some polite noise to fill the space. He laughs like he's heard the funniest joke in the history of jokes. He laughs and nearly drops the lasagna as he sets it on the table. He keeps laughing as he fetches a bottle of wine from the kitchen and pours me a glass. He spills it all over the table. He laughs until he's crying as he hands me the glass.

He gets me. How is it possible? In the history of human beings, Dez and BeeBee have managed to 'get me,' no one else. He pulls it together enough to speak, "It's good to see you too."

He kisses me on the cheek.

"The lasagna needs to rest. I drew a bath for you, should be perfect temp. Take your time, enjoy the wine. I'll check on you in half an hour." He turns and goes back to the kitchen. I stare at his beautiful hams flexing as he walks away. I wonder, because I must, if this is erotica, or if this is porn.

It doesn't matter. I'm officially falling in lust.

***

Lying on a beach, soaking in warm summer sun and cool ocean breezes. It's heaven, until a wave rolls in and crashes on top of me. Next thing you know, I'm gasping for air and choking on my own bath water. Not dreaming anymore.

Or am I? Is Detective-Too-Good-To-Be-True in my kitchen? Did he draw this bath, light these candles, and leave me in peace long enough for me to drown in my tub? A gentle knock on the door. He must have heard me doing the breaststroke. Before I say come in, he comes in. Not dreaming, not this part.

"You doin' okay in here?" He asks with such sweetness I feel guilty for thinking it's too much. But it is. We'll work on this later.

"Yeah, yeah, I'm fine. Seeing how much water I can get on the floor before the tub falls through it."

"Might not sit well with the neighbor."

"He's a bitch. Always complaining about how loud I walk. Fuck him."

I toss my hands in the air and give him my best 'who gives damn' face and end this part of the conversation with, "If he wanted quiet, he should have bought the penthouse."

"Since when is the fifth floor of anything the penthouse?"

Not sweet. This is better.

"If it's on the top, it's the penthouse. Prove me wrong."

"I'd rather feed you." He hands me a towel. He doesn't

leave. A dare.

I take the dare. I stand up, hang the towel over a hook, and grab my shower handle thing, what is it called? Shower handle, maybe? Whatever it is, I spray myself down, sending water everywhere. He gets wet and starts laughing. As God is my witness, his buttons will be pushed. He can't take everything in stride.

When I step out of the tub the room spins. He grabs me by the shoulders and guides my butt onto the toilet, which, thankfully is closed and does not have a candle on it.

"Sit still," he commands.

What? He takes the towel and starts drying me off. I know where this is going, at least for me. I have to stop this. I don't want to stop this. But I have to. We can't have sex, there's lasagna to be eaten. Lasagna is better than sex. But if you're going to have sex, having it before eating lasagna is better than after.

We are not having sex. Not tonight. And when we do, I won't talk about and I certainly won't write about it. I might mention it, I might even brag, but there won't be any details. This is neither porn nor erotica. Some things have to be private.

"I can handle it from here."

Disappointment flashes across his face. It didn't last long, but it was there. Good. He puts a hand on my cheek. His hand is warm, and soft, and big. He kisses me on my damp forehead and says, "Then hurry up, I'm hungry."

Laughing hurts my ribs and makes me stop. Then he laughs at me, which makes me laugh again. It's a hot mess of pain and happiness and arousal, and all sorts of other things running around inside my body and banging around my brain. Yes, yes, yes, a million times yes. This is the man for me.

"Get out before you kill me."

He pulls the towel over my head and walks out, still laughing. Quick as I can, I get dry, get dressed, and meet him at the table. There's a salad, the aforementioned lasagna, a bottle of wine, flowers, and candles. He must have gone shopping because none of this stuff came from my pantry. I'm not even sure I have a pantry. He pours the wine, lifts his glass, waits for me to lift mine and says, "Welcome home Charlie."

I pull my glass back "You said that already. Come up with something new."

"Geez, Charlie," he pretends to be annoyed. He's not annoyed. He's challenged and he likes it.

"Here's to not dying in a Dorothy costume in the parking lot of a seasonally gay nightclub."

That's more like it.

"Who said it was a costume?"

We drink. He sips, I gulp. Sucker. More for me.

We set down our glasses and he serves up the lasagna. He serves himself first. It's an interesting detail because the first serving is the worst. It's hard to get out of the pan, and looks a complete mess when you slap it onto a plate. I decide it's chivalry, not selfishness.

"Why?"

Of course I'm questioning his motives, I barely know him. I might be falling for him, and I might want to have his babies one day, but it's the journey we're on, not the destination we've reached.

"Why what?"

"All of this? You went to a lot of trouble. Why?"

"You could start with 'thank you' and then move on to questions?"

"You're right, thank you. This is not the evening I was expecting. It's thoughtful. I assume BeeBee told you my life story."

"No, he didn't. But he did tell me a lot. He called me today. He said you would most likely get home, skip dinner, and fall asleep in front of the TV. I thought you could do better for your first night home. I wanted to make it happen. By the way, he asked me to call him Brian."

BeeBee didn't tell me his real name until a month after we met. This is big. BeeBee (aka Brian Barkin) rarely tells anyone, outside of work, his actual name. It's a long story, but the quick version has two parts.

First, while he may be an estate attorney today, he started his career in the prosecutor's office. You never know, the guy you're getting cozy with could be the cousin of someone you sent to prison. It's the South, Atlanta's gay community isn't that big, it could happen.

Second, he's not a superstitious man, but he holds onto one unfounded belief. Giving out your first name gives away some of your power. I respect the first reason but the second one is bullshit. I'll believe it for the rest of my life, but I'll never tell him. What are friends for?

"How much time did you guys spend together?"

"We saw each other at the hospital a few times. Grabbed coffee there. Had dinner one time. Lunch once. No, twice. At first, I was surprised how open he was. Then I realized he was scared."

"Of what."

"Of losing you."

No way, BeeBee is the ultimate rogue lion. He needs no one. Least of all an about-to-fail-again writer. We're extremely close, but I can't imagine his life skipping even half a beat if I kicked the proverbial bucket. His emotional strength is a fair match for his physical strength, and he's a beast.

"Sweet, which is why it doesn't sound like BeeBee to me. He was pulling your leg."

He laughs with a mouth full of salad and nearly spits it

across the table at me. Disgusting, but forgivable under the circumstances. He swallows hard and I stare at the thick cords of his neck muscles descending into his shoulders, like El Capitan into the Yosemite Valley. Beautiful.

I'm a neck and shoulders guy. I like the whole enchilada, to be certain. But a not-too-thick neck on top of some nice beefy shoulders. Mmm, Mmm, good. Don't get me started on the nape of the neck, right below a nice short, perfectly faded, and preferably fresh, haircut. It's why I hate long hair. If I can't see your neck from behind, you're dead to me. If you have a mullet, I'll kill you.

I'm being dramatic. About the killing part. Everything else is legit.

Back to our conversation.

"Brian was not pulling my leg. He was chatty because he needed someone to talk to, about you. You're all he talked about. I would ask him about his work, he would talk about you. Mention the weather, he would talk about you. Asked him how he was doing, he talked about you. To be honest, it got boring."

Better be sarcasm. He sees the look on my face.

"All I'm saying is the guy cares about you. I get the feeling he doesn't have many close friends, and the ones he does have, they're intense for him."

I have to think about this for a minute.

BeeBee is my one true friend, possibly excepting Dez. We met in college. We had sex. It was his first time. My second. Or fifth. Not sure, lost count. Point is, it brought us closer. He went off to law school, we stayed in touch, spent holidays together when we weren't dating anyone (sometimes when we were). I'll admit it, I love BeeBee. Not in a 'let's get married, buy a house, order up some kids and settle down' way. That spark never happened between us. After all, my feelings for him kinda sorta got me into my current mess.

"BeeBee and I have a special relationship. It's not romantic, but it's more than platonic. Am I making sense?"

"Does it make sense to you?"

"Yes."

"Then it makes sense."

Can't argue with his logic. We eat in silence for a minute.

"Are you going to tell me?" I return to the interrogation.

"Tell you why I cleaned your place, made you dinner, etcetera, etcetera?"

"Yes, all of it."

"What do you think?"

"You're romancing the bone." Once again, I regret my words. Why does this happen to me? He doesn't laugh.

"Be serious. Why do you think I'd go to all this trouble?"

"Because you like me."

"Obvious. Keep going."

There's a lid for every pot.

"And because we have a deal."

"More than a deal, a pinky swear. I'm told it's a real commitment."

"You've researched it?"

"Called my niece. She's twelve. She confirms, pinky swears are unbreakable. Should we review our terms?"

I'm trapped. I have one last trick. Sincerity.

"Can we have the night as-is, and leave the details of my indiscretion for another time?"

It works. He lifts his glass, "To the night, as-is."

I lift mine, we toast, we drink.

We finish our dinner and move to the sofa, where I promptly fall asleep. I wake up with a blanket over me, and no Luke to be found. How do I know it was even real? Because he left the dishes for me. And I don't have a dishwasher.

You can't get more real.

CHAPTER FOUR

BeeBee has a Word

I didn't do the dishes when I woke up. It was around 11:00 p.m. and I knew I'd need an excuse not to write in the morning. I left them piled in the sink and went to bed, another problem solved.

In the morning, my first task, after the dishes, was to call BeeBee. He didn't answer. To be fair, I called his cell phone during business hours. He rarely answers. I called his office line, no answer. Then I remembered it's Friday and he doesn't go to the office on Friday. I'm desperate for a distraction. Anything to keep me away from my laptop.

Piedmont Park is a few blocks away and the weather is amazing and there's no way I'm taking a walk. Eggplant face, remember? I can't be seen like this. Stuck indoors, house is clean, leftovers in the fridge, no one to play with, and facing a deadline.

I'm about to surrender and sit at my nice desk, gifted to me by my publisher, when instead I call Luke. He left me this touching note:

Charlie,
Call me.

Luke

Literary genius. Of course it has his number, I'm not giving it out. It's coming up on noon. This day is not moving fast enough. I call him. He doesn't answer, I don't leave a message. What would I say? "Thanks for everything you did last night, sorry I passed out on the sofa." No, there are too many 'pleases' and 'thank yous' in the world already. I don't want to add to the noise.

I grab some leftovers and plant myself in front of the TV. Internet is out. Again. I try BeeBee's mobile. Still no answer. Nobody loves me today, and the universe is conspiring against me. I start to think Dez called God and said 'Keep an eye on the slacker for me.' Being an atheist wouldn't stop her.

I burn my mouth on my microwaved lunch because I'm an infant and don't understand the basic laws of thermodynamics. One more try with BeeBee. Zilch.

Somewhere around 1:30 I'm feeling bad enough for myself, I think I might be able to do some work. I open my laptop, fire up my favorite writing software (the free app included with the computer), select my favorite template, put my fingers on the keyboard, and… nothing.

My phone bursts to life with the best ringtone in the history of smartphones, "Fucking Best Song Ever." Saved. It's Dez. Not saved. I can't ignore the call, but I can be a bitch about the interruption. I can tell her truthfully, I'm working. She doesn't have to know nothing has been accomplished.

I get right to it. "Dez, can't talk, I'm working."

"Working? Then why do you keep calling BeeBee?"

Oops. Explains why he didn't answer. I go on the offensive.

"Whatever you two are up to, he better not bill me."

"Don't get snotty with me young man." She speaks with such dismissiveness and condescension, it's a reminder, as is her intent, why I love and respect her.

I am trapped by these people who know me too well. If

they didn't care, how much easier would life be?

"I'm not being snotty Auntie Dez, I am working, for reals. I'm sitting at my desk, the laptop is open and my fingers were on the keyboard when you called."

"Then why did you answer?"

She's got me there.

"I wanted to hear your apology."

She snorts out a sharp laugh.

"For what should I apologize?"

"You left me at the hospital. I had to take an Uber home. I hate Uber."

"Take Lyft next time. Or better yet, don't piss off your ride."

"It's me, come on."

"Touché. But no, no apology. Here's a life lesson for you Charlie. A forced apology is like a faked orgasm. Even if you pull it off, everyone goes away unsatisfied in the end."

Dez has the best life lessons.

My offensive falters. "Fine. What do you want?" I ask this with resignation. She hears it in my voice and, to my surprise, does not move in for the kill.

"CNN picked up our press release. They want an interview."

Hell no, not gonna happen. "Bad idea Dez."

"Why is it a bad idea?"

"Because I'm working."

"I didn't say this instant. You need the coverage."

"I look like crap."

"We can do a phone interview. We'll give them a nice pretty picture to paste up on the screen."

"Dez, please, no. They'll ask questions."

"It's called an interview for a reason."

"Questions I can't answer. Please," and she knows I hate to say please, and I said it twice, "can you stall them?"

"How long?"

Time to make another deal. I'm getting good at this.

"After I finish the book."

"Perfect. December seventh it is."

She's thrilled and it takes me a second to realize what happened. I agreed to kick off a marketing campaign for a book I don't have. I start to speak and realize she's hung up on me.

My day of infamy awaits.

I suck at this.

***

"Lucy, I'm home…"

It's BeeBee. He never knocks. If he knocked, he would give me the option of telling him to go away. He never knocks.

I hear bags rustling and his footsteps as he walks toward the kitchen. I get up from my desk and head to the kitchen, hoping he's brought ice cream with him. We have this thing, BeeBee and I, about food. We like to eat our feelings. Since I'm a cold-hearted bitch, I like ice cream. BeeBee's more of a mac-n-cheese guy.

We meet in the kitchen and… no ice cream. What the hell?

"Shouldn't you be working?" and it comes out snippier than I planned, but I don't care. Again, no ice cream. He gives me a look like a librarian staring at me over her glasses right after I've made some lewd or disgusting sound. But he doesn't wear glasses.

"Are you calling me black?"

"What?" I am lost.

"Do I have to spell it out for you, Mister Pot?" he asks, and returns to emptying bags.

"I've been working. Trying to work. I keep getting interrupted."

"Do you want me to leave?"

"It's good to see you BeeBee. I do not want you to leave. But you didn't bring..." and he cuts me off.

"There's ice cream in your freezer. You'd know if you ever opened it."

Luke. We never made it to dessert.

"Luke was concerned about your lack of nourishment. This should hold you over for a few days, at least until you can stand to be seen in public."

If he spoke to Luke...

"Did you see him today?"

"We had lunch. And before you get all twisted about it, I'm not after your man and I didn't set it up. It was Dez's idea."

"Sounds like a conspiracy. What are you plotting?"

"The resurrection of your career, the protection of your future, your personal safety, all the boring shit you should be doing for yourself, but can't be bothered to manage."

"Big project. How's it working out for you?"

For reasons unbeknownst to me, he becomes angry. At me. He raises his voice and starts swearing, which is a good sign he's angry.

"What do you think we're doing here? You think this is a game? You need to grow up. Your snarky-ass 'I don't give a shit' bullshit is startin' to wear pretty thin."

"BeeBee...Brian...what do you want me to say..."

"How about thank you, bitch," he shouts in my face.

He's close enough I can see his eyes are moist. Maybe it's stress tears, or maybe something else.

It cuts me to the bone. He's cried in front of me exactly once, when his mother died. I cannot be number two on his list.

I put up my hands and slowly move them to his shoulders. He doesn't pull away. Which is good. He's too close to punch me.

"Take a deep breath and let's talk. Let's push the reset

button on this conversation. I'll start, okay?"

"I'm listening."

A joke comes to mind and I swat it away like it's an angry wasp. I know better.

"We both know you're right. I am a terrible person. I'm self-focused, cold hearted, and my jokes are always in poor taste. I've always believed those were things you liked about me, cute things that make our relationship work."

He isn't receiving my words quite the way I hoped.

"Charlie dammit..." he says, under his breath, his teeth grinding.

"What I'm trying to tell you is I'm grateful. For you, for Dez, for everything you do for me. If you need me to change, I'll change."

I let this sink in. For some reason he's full-on crying. Am I doing this wrong? Nowhere to go but forward.

"Brian, I don't have anyone else. You're my family. It's the truth and you know it."

It's Niagara Falls. Tears, quivering lips, runny nose. I wanted to make him feel better. Honesty is supposed to be the best policy, right? Since my attempt is turning into an epic failure, I'm about to stop talking. Then he hugs me. More than hugs, constricts. He wraps those big arms around me, sticks his face in my neck, and squeezes the breath out of me. He's forgotten about my ribs.

"You scared the shit outta me Charlie," he whispers into my neck.

The defenses fall away, all shields are down. My eyes are burning. My face is wet. I tell myself it's the bear hug he's got me in, but I know it's more.

"I know. I'm sorry. I promise I'll never get beat up again."

Either he laughed or blew his nose on my shirt. Fine either way. As much as it's hurting me, I don't want this moment to end. Not yet.

I don't think I've scared the shit out of anyone before. If it happened, I missed it. He released me from his death grip, helped me put away the groceries, then made me sit and listen. It's hard to listen. I normally don't care what anyone has to say.

We sit at the table and he tells me all about Halloween night. It seems like another lifetime. He didn't realize the extent of my injuries. He thought it was a busted nose, no big deal. To be fair, I didn't know how bad things were either. Officer Goode got the full picture. Slamming the back of your head into the pavement makes everything worse. Much worse. Like a week in the hospital worse.

Someone who knows someone else who knows BeeBee saw me get strapped onto a gurney and hauled away unconscious. They got word to BeeBee. It's amazing how fast bad news can travel through a crowd, and find its way to its rightful owner.

The club, Xanadu, is a stand-alone building with two parking lots, an upper and a lower. For Halloween, they turn the lower parking lot into an extension of the club, weather permitting. While it rained during the day, it wasn't much and the outdoor party went on unimpeded. Glinda, being eleven feet tall, couldn't fit through any of the doors. She partied with the lower parking lot throng, dancing to her own beat.

Finding Glinda took zero effort.

Moments after hearing about my method of departure, Glinda rushed back to the scene of my demise and located Luke. Luke, being a cop, was interviewing witnesses. To my utter astonishment, he found some. There were plenty to find, but I can't believe any self-respecting gay man would push the pause button on his Halloween debauchery long enough to talk to a cop about some strangers in a fist fight, one-sided or not.

It's more a testament to Officer Goode's looks and charm, than anything to do with being a good citizen. Yes, I am a cynic. I mean, nobody's a good citizen when they're in drag, right? Luke could be an exceptional cop, which explains why he's a detective. Nonsense. His looks won the day. I like my first version better.

Picture the scene, an eleven-foot-tall Glinda the Good Witch strides through the throng of costumed revelers, towers over a cop, and waits until she's noticed. It doesn't take long. BeeBee relays the conversation to me, of course it's an accurate retelling. Judge for yourself.

Good Witch Glinda is noticed by Officer Goode, who says, "Glinda, I'm glad you're here. I want to talk to you."

To which Glinda replies, "Where did they take him?"

"Grady."

"Why not Emory?"

"There's no trauma unit at Emory."

"He needs a trauma unit?"

"The EMTs made the call."

Glinda spins and marches away, swearing to herself, "Dammit, dammit, dammit."

She opens the back of her rented SUV, Glinda owns a car but decided we needed to go big for Halloween, she rented an Escalade. She proceeds to transform into Brian Barkin in the parking lot. I can imagine the audience reaction. More precisely, I can imagine the show. Glinda/Brian is unashamed of her/his body and has no reason to be. BeeBee spent his childhood playing Rugby and swimming naked in the sea with his friends, nudity is no big deal. He didn't grow up with the body shame many people carry. Lucky him.

For the record, I don't care who sees me naked either. Just sayin'.

Besides, it was more expedient to change there. The plan was to stay at my place after the party; a change of clothes was on hand. Eleven-foot Glinda became virtually-naked BeeBee, then quickly made the final transition to Brian, albeit with sparkly makeup still in place. He jumped into the SUV and off he went, chasing the ambulance, as it were.

Xanadu the club, not Kublai Khan's summer place, is on the east side of Atlanta. It's not a gay club but it goes full gay for special occasions, like Halloween, Mardi Gras, and Saint Patrick's Day. Yes, we have Mardi Gras in Atlanta, but without the parades. Parades are useless. Unless it's Pride, then hurray for parades.

Xanadu is not far from Grady Hospital, as the crow flies. But it's a lot closer to Emory Hospital, in terms of drive time. Interstate 85 cuts right through the middle of the city, and it makes a big curve around Grady Hospital. Being creative types here in the South, we named this section of highway 'The Grady Curve.'

I tell you all this because I want you to understand the scope of what he did. Getting to Grady Hospital from Xanadu, unless you're equipped with lights and sirens, or wings, is not easy. If it weren't for one wrong turn, Brian would have made it to the hospital before the ambulance.

It's a good thing he took out insurance on the rental. Escalades aren't built for jumping curbs. Or driving over road signs, through garbage cans, bashing into guard rails, or for any of the craziness Brian told me he did. Thankfully by this point in his story we were laughing and drinking and behaving like our old selves.

I wish he'd stopped there. I didn't need to know what happened next.

I did need to know. But I didn't want to know. I'm sure it's why he told me. It's not enough I know how he felt. I need to know what he went through. His opinion, not mine. For me, we already arrived at the conclusion of the chapter. We're good.

Before I go further, it's OK. It's not the worst thing in the world. Well, not for me, I was unconscious. For BeeBee it was the continuation of a bad night. Nobody died, nobody (else) got beat up, no one went to jail. None of it. But all of it came close. I imagine such things can be stressful.

BeeBee arrived at Grady fresh on the heels of the ambulance. It was a busy night, but they started on me right away. This is a good time for a shout-out to the good peeps at the Grady Hospital ER. It's always busy there, but Halloween is a special night in hospital emergency rooms, and not in a good way. Mix in a full moon, and the weirdness sets in real fast. Glad to say we were ahead of the curve, arriving before the crush of patients they were expecting. To their credit, even though the night was young and the place wasn't quite yet insane, the doctors and nurses did not tell jokes at my expense.

I would not have shown such restraint.

Lest you've forgotten, blue gingham dress, pinned-on wig with ponytails and bows, makeup, ruby red Mary Janes, and fake boobs.

By the way, do you have any idea how hard it is to find ruby red Mary Janes in a man's size thirteen? I searched for days. I finally got smart about it and went to a discount shoe store on the edge of Midtown, an area we affectionately refer to as our 'gayborhood.' A nice sales lady smiled at me and said, "Of course we have those sugar, all the ladies get their shoes from us." She said 'sugar' as a true Southerner would say it, "ShooGuh." She also told me which glitter to use to make them sparkle like Dorothy's. Southerners are such nice folks.

Back to Team Grady. They were amused, of course. Probably had lots of laughs at my expense over drinks after their shift ended. I became a part of Grady Halloween lore. I'm glad to have been of service. They deserve some good laughs. It makes up for Hurricane BeeBee.

They didn't want him hanging around while they sorted me out. He didn't want to take a seat and wait. He wanted to be right there in the mix, and he wasn't taking no for an answer. He's good at not taking no for an answer.

It was a bad idea.

Grady is one of two public hospitals with a trauma center in the entire northern half of the state of Georgia. It's a lot to ask of a hospital. They get everything; shootings, stabbings, car accidents, plane crashes, beat up Dorothys, you name it. If it's bad, it goes to Grady.

They have excellent security.

Which is who they called when things got heated and BeeBee asserted, loudly, he wasn't going anywhere. He was all emotion. Once he lost it, a couple of guys in uniform showed up and made their intentions as clear as he had made his.

It was about to get ugly. It was about to get physical. Somebody was about to get beat up. Somebody was about to go to jail. And it's quite possible I was about to die.

None of it happened.

None of it happened because, as the two security guards were deciding whether or not to forcibly remove BeeBee, Officer Luke Goode in his Atlanta Police Department uniform arrived on the scene.

BeeBee stopped yelling and cursing long enough to stare down Officer Goode and, thinking he was about to get arrested, did the smartest thing he could come up with at the time. He dialed up the heat and asked, "What the hell do you want?"

I'm pretty sure the two security guards thought this was it for BeeBee. Instead, Luke holds out a small, misshapen and damp stuffed toy dog with Velcro stitched to its side and says, "I found Toto."

A few moments of stunned silence followed, then another discovery related to my costume was made. A male nurse, removing my ruby red slippers asked, loud enough for all present to hear "What the hell is this?"

BeeBee's head whips around like a weather vane in a tornado. He lays eyes on the nurse. The nurse, with a mix of rage and wonder, is staring at my shoes, and his own two hands, sparkling red in the bright lights of the ER. Ruby-red glitter was everywhere, and spreading like the plague.

In his deep baritone voice, tinged with his best bitchy-queen inflection, BeeBee, in full Good Witch makeup, shouts, "It's glitter bitch, deal with it."

Which is absurd. You can't deal with glitter. Once you get glitter, you always have glitter. There's no reasoning with glitter. Glitter is how I show people I love them at Christmas, I only send cards with glitter to people I never want to see again. I hate glitter. I carried those shoes in a sealed bag until we got to the party, fully intending to throw them away when we left. Yes, it is wasteful and environmentally unfriendly. Can you forgive me?

Anyway, someone laughed. The tension was broken.

Toto and my ruby red slippers, the one-two punch saved the night from getting a lot worse.

A smart young ER doc made a snap decision. She pointed at the floor across from the space in which I'm being examined and says, "See those floor tiles? Pick 12 and get in 'em. If you promise to stay there, you can stay there."

Without another word, BeeBee took up residence in twelve square feet of floor space up against the wall. Three feet by four feet, in case you're not a math whiz. It ain't much. Luke, without being asked or instructed, did the same. Their vigil didn't last long. I was taken away for imaging, then to the ICU.

It didn't get much better from there, not for BeeBee.

It also didn't get any worse.

***

As it turned out, the trauma center was the correct call. I suspect probably-lesbian EMT had my best interests in mind when she made her decision. Better safe than sorry. Or she thought a guy in a dress would be better received at Grady. I could find out her name and ask her, and thank her. No, such behavior would be out of character for me.

Whatever the reason, she may have saved my life.

If I ever see her again, I'll offer to buy her a Bud Light. Or three, or six, or ten. I bet she shoots pool. I bet she's good at it. I could start hanging out at bars with pool tables and lesbians and hope to run into her one day. I'm sure there's one around here someplace. Dare to dream. None of it matters, other than I'm glad I landed where I did and I have her and her EMT partner to thank for it.

Because my favorite TV doctor works at Grady.

Not a TV doctor in the fake-ass Dr. What's-his-name-I-don't-wanna-get-sued TV doctor mode. Let's call him Bill. Dr. Bill is not licensed to practice squat. I don't hate the man, I'm drawing a distinction between him and Dr. Sanjay Gayakwad. Do not make fun of his name, his is the ninety-fourth most common surname in India, look it up. Dr. Gayakwad is a for-real kick-ass-and-take-names neurosurgeon. He did ad-hoc brain surgery in a war zone. Top that, Bill.

Dr. Bill wants you to talk about your feelings. Useless.

Dr. Gayakwad the neurosurgeon works at Grady Hospital. I didn't get to meet him. A couple days after I arrived, he stopped by to see me in the ICU, I'd say more as a novelty than a medical necessity. He'd seen the news about me, because, duh, he works for a global media conglomerate, and wanted to see me in the flesh.

I found out later he read my first book, a serious book about my misspent youth in Texas, and was shocked at the subject and tone of my second book. He, like everyone else who bought the second book, found the transition from one to the next jarring. Tough shit, I'm an artist, it's art, judge not lest ye be judged.

BeeBee was there, I know this happened.

Dr. Gayakwad walks into the ICU, chats with a nurse, comes into my room, and does not say boo to BeeBee. He nods, smiles, then looks down at me, all bashed up and unconscious, looks back at BeeBee and says, "I see he's as good a fighter as he is a writer." He then laughs at his own joke and walks out. My kinda guy. Too bad I wasn't awake for it.

He stepped back in a couple minutes later and asked, "Are you family?"

To which BeeBee immediately replied, "Yes."

"I see the resemblance. Listen, he's gonna be OK. You should get some rest. I know tired when I see it."

Then he walked out again, this time for good. Never came back, never checked in again, nothing. BeeBee found this reassuring.

I might send him a refund, assuming he bought the books and didn't borrow them from the library. I think the paperbacks are going for a buck fifty on the discount shelf at Farnes & Boble.

Not long after this celebrity check-in, Luke made his first follow-up appearance in the ICU. BeeBee swears by all things holy I was awake for part of this, and I will believe him because it's easier than arguing. I know how to choose my battles, especially with BeeBee.

When Luke arrived, BeeBee had stepped out to chat with Nurse Gale about coffee.

BeeBee has a way of getting people to break rules and

make exceptions for him. I know from personal experience. I don't begrudge him this talent, I envy him for it. A note about envy. I don't see it as a sin, certainly not a deadly sin. I like envy. Envy is motivational for me. I don't care about material things much, I never envy someone's watch or car or big bank account.

I envy their skill, their talent, their ability. If you can do something I can't, and I envy it, I will haunt your life until I learn how to do the same, or you figure out how to permanently ditch me.

I have never been able to match BeeBee's ability to get whatever he wants, from whomever he chooses, once he sets his mind to it. His experience in the ER notwithstanding. He got his way, didn't he? I rest my case.

You may be wondering why BeeBee had to use his special powers to get a cup of coffee. It's simple, he grew up drinking Jamaican Blue Mountain coffee. He was weened of his momma's milk with the stuff. Jamaican Blue Mountain coffee is, hands down, the best coffee in the world. If you argue with me on this point you will lose. If you argue with BeeBee on this point, he'll brew a cup for you. If you continue to argue, he'll never speak to you again.

It's delicious, enjoy.

When I came back from a vacation to the island with five pounds of fresh roasted, 100% pure Jamaican Blue Mountain whole coffee beans, and presented them to BeeBee, you would've thought I was handing him his first-born child. His joy was resplendent.

BeeBee is a coffee snob, through and through. BeeBee has also been forced to drink more than his fair share of the worst coffee on earth, which is any coffee brewed in an institutional setting. Office, university, courthouse, all those places with a coffee 'service' where they burn the crap out of it in some dark, dingy room, using equipment unwashed since the invention of time. Every sip tastes like remorse.

From his lengthy experience, BeeBee learned most institutions, including hospitals, had coffee snobs like him on staff. These like-minded people tended to secret away special coffee makers, and brewed their own cups of superior grade joe. This is why BeeBee was using his charm on Nurse Gale. This is also why he was distracted when Luke arrived. It didn't take long for Nurse Gale to cave, and before you know it, she's leading BeeBee to the coffee promised land.

The ICU has a couple rooms where nurses and doctors can grab some shuteye. In one of these rooms, the indigenous coffee snobs of the ICU had erected a shrine to coffee. Their drug of choice? Counter Culture Coffee. Counter Culture roasts up special blends and single source beans and gives them cool names like 'Big Trouble,' 'Hologram,' 'Fast Forward,' and, BeeBee's new personal favorite, 'forty-six.' I don't know why it's his favorite, accept it.

While BeeBee was off getting his fix with Nurse Gale, Luke arrived at my bedside. With Toto. A crappy toy dog I got at the thrift store on North Avenue had taken on significance for Luke. It's charming, but I don't get it. But there he was, holding the dog, looking down at me, with those pretty blue eyes of his.

I mention his eyes because I'm told I spoke to Luke about them. Allegedly I said, "Your eyes are like laser beams etching your name on my soul."

Bull. Shit. I did not say those words. There is no universe in the multiverse in which I said those words. Unless there's an audio or video recording of the incident, I will never acknowledge I said those words. It's okay, I have plausible deniability, good enough for me. Whatever I said, it made Luke laugh. He's standing there, holding Toto, looking down at me, and laughing. At me. This is when BeeBee returns.

"What's going on? Why are you laughing?" BeeBee's

hackles are up, he's in Charlie defense mode.

"You won't believe what he said to me," he tells him as he's still laughing.

I'm sad to report BeeBee did believe him. After Luke repeats this maudlin nonsense, they're both laughing. Is it okay to laugh like this in the ICU? Let's take a vote. I say no. Nurse Gale agrees with me, consider carefully before you decide. True, she didn't like the volume. I didn't like being the cause of the commotion. Different criteria, but we arrived at the same vote.

BeeBee was worried he might lose his special coffee privileges, of course he had to share the joke with Nurse Gale when she walked in and told them to lower the volume. All three are laughing and drawing attention. A doctor comes along and tells them to keep it down. The doctor is angry. Nurse Gale is oh-so-sorry. BeeBee tries to stifle it. Luke is embarrassed. According to all present, I, without raising my head, shouted, "Laughter is the best medicine."

You might say it was a bonding moment for everyone, except the doctor.

The friendship between BeeBee and Luke started in earnest then, and lead BeeBee to tell Luke his real name, among other things. Luke convinced BeeBee to go home and rest. He would stay with me until visiting hours were over.

Which is what he did. I wonder what we talked about?

I have another question.

This is the question I have. If I said the things they say I said, what things did I say which they, or at least Luke, aren't telling me about? Did I profess my love for Cheetos and Rocky Road ice cream while taking massive bong hits?

I hate all three of those things. I'm not against pot. I'm against smoking. Anything. How nuts do you have to be to intentionally suck toxic filth into your lungs, then blow it out for others to breathe in? But hey, who am I to judge? As for

THC, I think it's best when eaten.

Did I confess this to Luke in my delirium? Boxers or briefs? Did we have such a chat? Luke had about three hours alone with me and I have no recollection of what went on. And it happened more than once. Yes, I have things to hide. Lots of things.

Like how all this happened.

I know you know I have my secrets. Unless you've been skipping pages or speed-reading. I may never know the answer to my question. But I can make some educated guesses.

CHAPTER FIVE

A Lesson in Process

Luke and BeeBee came up with an overlapping visiting schedule, wrapped around their respective work schedules. They made a spreadsheet. It had pivot tables and hidden panels and formulas, all the crap you need in order to visit a friend in the hospital. They looped in Dez, in case she wanted to participate, which she did. Once. Twice, if you count the day she didn't drive me home.

I remember her visit to the ICU. It's one of those exploding memory bombs from the day I regained most of my wits, on day five. She was there on day three. Didn't come back until day seven. Who can blame her? It's no exaggeration to say it was a shit-show.

This is what I remember. I could be completely wrong. I haven't talked to Dez about it, and I won't, ever. This is how I recall the event and I have no desire to have anyone else confirm or refute it.

Before I get into the gory details, I think a lesson in 'process' is in order. I never knew any of this before. I'm sharing it with you because, as they say, sharing is caring.

Here we go.

There are three ways a patient can have a bowel movement in the ICU.

Look, if you don't want to know about this, skip to the next chapter. I suggest you stick with me, you never know when this type of information will come in handy. I wish I knew about this before I experienced it first-hand. In truth, I'm doing you a favor.

Three ways.

First, you can shit the bed. Nobody wants this, but it happens. Nurses do not get paid enough to deal with this, and doctors aren't about to deal with it. This, while first on our ordered list, is last on the 'let's do it' list.

Second, you can poop in a bed pan. Not quite as messy, but someone still has to deal with your mess, and, unless you have a specific fetish, this is not something a trained professional wants to manage. Plus, somebody's gotta wipe. Do you wanna wipe someone else's ass? Me neither.

Before I go further, I want to acknowledge there are people who have been required to do these things, who are not paid professionals, but have been tasked with the care of a loved one and had to do it. I hope whoever they took care of left them a mountain of cash in their will because, damn, they earned it.

On to number three. A BMS system. Bowel Management System. OK, this sounds reasonable, right? A system whereby one's bowels are managed. To me, this should be a system which, by way of magic, automatically precludes the need for a dump in the first place.

No such luck. BMS is a euphemism for a tube up your ass. You read it right, a tube, up your ass. There's more to it, like a seal, and suction, and… you get the picture, and if you don't, there's a YouTube video created by a cute young nurse down Australia way - go for it. As far as I know, option number one did not happen. I'm not saying it didn't happen, I'm saying if it did, no one told me. Option number two also did not happen, because I'd have been awake for it.

Option number three.

It's possible, again I'm not saying it happened, it's possible the deployment of the BMS was triggered by some incident. If I were a religious sort, I would thank God every day for my ignorance of this. But I'm not religious, let's move on. The BMS system. I become aware of a tube up my ass bright and early on day three of my sojourn.

Desiree Adalicia Masters, as everyone knows, is a morning person. She loves to rise before the sun, run a few miles, crush a few souls, drink a hot cup of tea, and head off to the office. She arrives at 7:00am. Desiree Adalicia Masters lives in a swanky part of town called 'Tuxedo Park,' a few minutes away from her office in Buckhead, a city unto itself spitting distance from Atlanta proper. She does not suffer the hideous commute of the wretched masses, who troop into the city every day from the burbs hoping they don't die in a terrible car crash along the way. Which means she has time for a healthy breakfast.

Still, the fact anyone would be anywhere, other than in bed, at 7:00 a.m. is, to my mind, idiotic.

Day three was a Sunday. She didn't have to be anywhere on Sunday. Atheist, remember? It was raining. Nonetheless, the intrepid Mrs. Masters decided to drive down the largely empty Peachtree Street from Buckhead into Atlanta to come and see me.

Visiting hours start at 9:00 a.m. Naturally, she was early. It was close to 9:00 a.m., they sent her on up. This is important.

Because at 8:30 a.m. I'm having a heated debate with a nurse and a doctor, it takes two of them for this, along the lines of 'get this whatever it is out of my ass before I pull it out myself.' Charming, right? Here are these dedicated medical professionals who probably thought the day would be like any other day on the job, trying desperately to get me to calm down, in the nicest way possible.

They threatened to strap me to the bed.

Orderlies were called in to assist.

What's worse than having a tube up your ass? Being strapped to a bed with a tube up your ass. If this turns you on, please burn this book and never speak to me, ever. I'm not judging you, but I do not want to know you.

I calmed down. I did more than calm down. I went from demanding to begging. I'm not proud of it, but I wanted the tube out of my ass. I was going to try every trick in my book to get the job done. I might have been channeling BeeBee. It worked. At 8:45 a.m., the good doctor and nurse agreed to remove the tube. They kept the orderlies on hand, in case. The room was already crowded. Too crowded. I don't blame them for staying, I gave them good reason. You might say I opened the door to it.

At 8:50 a.m., the removal process began.

This involves the patient, me, rolling onto their side and following the doctor's order to 'try to relax.' There's some fumbling about, some peeling of an adhesive thingy, the seal, some tugging, and some carefully timed deep inhales and exhales.

At 8:58 a.m., the deed was almost done. The tip was all that remained. I'm on my side, a doctor and a nurse are pulling a tube out of my ass, two orderlies are in the room to do, what else, ensure order. I hope they enjoyed the show.

It was exactly 8:59 a.m. when Desiree Adalicia Masters walked into my room.

She pushed right through the door. I know the exact time because I was facing the door, and I saw a big red digital clock over the nurses' station. Why I chose to focus attention there is a mystery we'll never solve.

What followed happened in slow motion, but transpired in

a matter of seconds.

She walks in and stops cold. I'm essentially naked. My paper-thin gown is hiked up to allow the team to do their duty and Desiree Adalicia Masters gets the full Monty. This wasn't a big deal, we're both adults, all good. But I don't like a non-medical audience when I'm having my BMS removed.

She walks into the room, I'm startled, which startled the doctor. Or the nurse, not sure who was doing what at this point. This in turn startles both of the orderlies, one of whom bumps into the active participant behind me, who in turn stabs me in the ass with the BMS. This hurts. Insert whatever gay joke you want in this spot, I'm saying this hard plastic object jabbing into my ass, at an angle, hurt. Have some empathy.

I instinctively pulled away from what hurts, wouldn't you?

The tube pops out, gets fumbled, makes a strange gurgling noise, and whoosh, my shit flies across the room and splatters across Desiree Adalicia Masters' beautiful white jeans.

There are two things about this.

First, I know what you're thinking, what the hell is she doing wearing white in what is clearly the first week of November? I can speculate. If I know my publisher, she thought something like, 'It's a hospital, I'll wear white, it will be fashionable and I'll fit right in.'

The second thing to know is it wasn't a lot. It wasn't like a shit version of Carrie. It was a small spurt, like somebody stepped on one of those fast-food packages of ketchup, but it contained shit instead of ketchup. Try not to think of this the next time you go out for a burger. I dare you.

Someone behind me shouts, "Oh my god" and I'm practically climbing out of the bed, trying get away from the evil tube before I suffer the same fate as Desiree Adalicia Masters. Why do I keep using her full name? Because, dignity. I want to give her some shred of dignity.

She's my publisher, she might read this someday.

For her part, Desiree Adalicia Masters didn't say a word. She gagged. Once, then twice, then bam, out it came. She puked, a geyser's worth. She put the kid from "The Exorcist" to shame. She puked everywhere. On the floor. All over my bed. All across my legs. On one of the orderlies, who took it surprisingly well. Apparently, this happens to orderlies all the time. God bless 'em all.

Once she finished her venting procedure, she turned and ran from the room. I don't know where she went. The door closed behind her. I could hear lots of noise, shouting, crying. It was as though everyone in the room, except me, tried to get out of the room at the same time.

The puked-upon orderly promptly slipped and fell, causing the second orderly to back into a corner, allowing the nurse to then fall over the first orderly, landing with a sound I, for good reason, found funny. It was this strange squishy-splatty sound, like a kid stomping in a mud puddle. Yes, I laughed.

The doctor was trapped and when you thought it couldn't get worse, a well-meaning nurse rushing to the room to render aid, or to see what insanity was taking place, shoved open the door. The door struck the nurse in the back as she was trying to stand up. She wasn't hurt, but she did do a face plant into the puked-upon orderly's crotch.

Desiree Adalicia Masters did not return to the hospital until the day of my discharge. I can't say as I blame her. And I'm no fashion genius, but I'm fairly certain she'll never wear white to a hospital again. I also believe there is no amount of red wine she can drink to ever get her to speak of this.

Unless she starts seeing her therapist again. I should probably do something nice for her. But I digress, again. I can't help myself.

***

* * *

Back to me and BeeBee in my kitchen.

He told me all about his visits to see me in the hospital, and his dates with Luke. He made dinner, we started drinking and laughing and carrying on like college kids. I might have told him about Dez's visit. And yes, I said 'dates.' What else can you call them?

The two of them would make plans, then follow through on those plans. Those are dates, play dates, as opposed to romantic dates, or hookups, but dates by definition. I wasn't jealous. BeeBee already said he wasn't after 'my man.' I also had this notion, from the welcome home dinner Luke put together, Luke was into me.

And Luke said all BeeBee talked about was me. All good. Not jealous. Until the next morning. BeeBee stayed the night. Normally, BeeBee would sleep in my bed with me. It's not sexual, two gay guys can sleep in the same bed without having sex, as easily as two straight guys.

It's easier for straight guys to share a bed without having sex, assuming they're not drunk and neither one is a closeted gay. If even one of them is fake-straight, and they're both 'wasted dude,' then sex can happen pretty easily. Been there, done that. Not how it is with me and BeeBee.

I happen to have a giant bed, a California King. It's extra-long, it accommodates giants like BeeBee. He asked me to buy one, and I did. When he spends the night, which is not often, he sleeps with me. We're like two puppies snuggled up in a crate. It's sweet.

I'm not kidding, there's no sex. Get your mind out of the gutter.

He did not sleep in my bed. I'm a light sleeper normally, and because my ribs were still a bit sore and I needed the space to myself, he slept on the sofa. BeeBee can sleep through an earthquake.

No joke, he was staying with me one weekend while his place was being painted. There was a nasty car accident in the street in front of my building. I woke up, ran to the balcony, and looked down in time to see some guy in boxers wearing an open powder blue bathrobe get out of his wrecked car. A Toyota Corolla hatchback was wrapped, like detritus after a flood, around a telephone pole. The bathrobe guy reached into the front seat, grabbed a small dog, a real one, not stuffed, then ran off into the night in fuzzy pink slippers. I was not hallucinating, it happened, it was real, and it was noisy.

A crowd gathered, sirens wailed, firetrucks and police cars arrived. The flatbed car hauler was the loudest of them all, with its insistent 'beep, beep, beep' which doesn't turn off until the damn thing is in drive. I stayed on my balcony for the entire show. When I went back to bed, BeeBee hadn't stirred one bit. The next day, he claimed he heard nothing.

Back to the present, asleep in bed with deep-sleeper BeeBee out cold on the sofa.

My place is old and has high ceilings. There's not a stitch of carpet because carpet is gross, and old places should be spared the indignity of fabric flooring. Wood floors throughout. Noise travels in my place. When BeeBee's phone started ringing at 7:00 a.m., I assumed it was my phone, and Dez was calling me. In other words, I tried to ignore it. It kept ringing. Eventually I woke up enough to realize it couldn't be my phone because, duh, it's not playing my song. I got up and went to find the phone, presumably BeeBee's. Not to answer it. Hell no, to shut it off.

I have this small wood table with glass on top by my front door. Some people would call it a demi table, but us fancy gays know it's called a demi-lune table. Consider yourself enlightened. I drop all my crap there when I get home. It's a messy pile of spare change, bills for me to ignore, letters I'm never going to answer, keys, and, in the middle of all this, my phone charger.

BeeBee left his phone there, on my charger, as he often does when he visits. He has never asked permission, and never needs to. It's a charger, why would he?

Before I got to it, it stopped ringing. Yay, mission accomplished. Until I heard the 'plink' sound signaling a text message. I thought, "Screw it, I'm awake, might as well see who it is." At this point it was low risk. Whoever sent it wouldn't know if I read it. No interaction required. I reasoned it might be something important enough to wake the Sleeping Giant.

It was from Luke. It said, 'Looking forward to this morning.'

Am I dreaming? Did I pick up my phone? No, I'm looking at BeeBee's phone. I know this because BeeBee has the same case as me, I bought it for him, except his has purple trim and mine has blue trim. I also know this because Luke is not in my contacts. His name would not show up in the message.

Somewhere in the back of my head, a bell started ringing. An itty-bitty sound from far away. Not like the Bells of Notre Dame, more like the bells of an antique fire truck, far in the distance, and approaching. The kind Dalmatians rode on when firemen had to manually pump the water.

I'm not the jealous type. I am the 'I'm lonely and haven't had a proper date in a long time and would like to get laid type.' This is a good time for an exception to my rule, but I decide not to go there. BeeBee and Luke are becoming friends. I should be happy. I should encourage it, since I, as I mentioned, want to have Luke's babies. Yes, I know I can't have his babies, not in this version of the universe. I like saying it. Aren't I clever?

I dismiss the bells and put the phone down. Then I go back to bed. I could wake BeeBee up, because clearly, he's going to miss his morning meet-up with Luke. But I don't. It's one thing to accept their friendship, another thing entirely to facilitate it.

CHAPTER SIX

Taking Stock

Let's pause and take stock of the situation.

I got shit-stomped and taken to the hospital while wearing a Dorothy costume. For any non-Southerner who happens to read this, 'shit-stomped' means beat up real bad. As okay as I am with men wearing dresses, or women wearing pants, I don't like the fact I ended up having mine cut off in the emergency room.

I spent a week in the hospital. Not the hospital, the ICU. And the handsome blue-eyed devil of a cop I have a thing for is having dates with my best friend.

Oh yeah, and I have a book to write by the end of the month. Haven't started it, not a word.   Normally in a situation like this I would find a distraction. A walk in the park, a hookup, day drinking at Henry's, anything away from my desk.

Henry isn't a person. Henry is a dog. There's a restaurant/bar a couple blocks away named after him. I like the place, the bartenders like me too, and tend to pour heavy for me. Or they don't like me, and are secretly trying to kill me with alcohol. Doesn't matter to me, I get what I want either way, a stiff drink in the company of handsome men. What better way to spend the afternoon. Sundays are the best days for day drinking because you get to call it brunch and nobody thinks you're a loser.

I'm not doing any of it. I'm not doing anything because I look terrible. I don't feel terrible, not physically. But I can't shake this notion I might have missed an opportunity with a nice guy, and my best friend happened to be there to scoop up the opportunity. Like the guy who drops a $20 bill on the sidewalk and doesn't realize it until he goes to pay for his coffee and donuts ten minutes later. The person who comes along and finds the twenty gets to keep it.

I have a choice. I've had lots of those lately. This time, I can choose to let the $20 go, or I can retrace my steps and try to find it. I wrestle with this decision for all of thirty seconds. After this taking-stock exercise, I realize the best thing to come out of this mess is Luke.

I have another decision. Do I care if BeeBee and Luke are striking up more than a friendship, and if I do, do I want to disrupt it? Easy answer, yes, I care and damn right I'm gonna disrupt it. I saw him first. He's my money, and I want him now. I don't care who finds him.

I've settled it, I need a plan of action. I suck at plans. I can barely read a plan, much less create one. I tend to rely on BeeBee for plans. How would our conversation go down? "Hey, BeeBee, you know how you're always managing my life and fixing my problems? Yeah, like, how do you think I should break up this budding romance between you and my future husband?"

Dez can help me. "Hey Dez, I need some relationship advice. If I think BeeBee is makin' a move on Luke while I'm recuperating from my injuries. What should I do?" To which I'm sure she would respond with all kinds of motherly, no, sisterly advice.

If I didn't owe her a book.

See? I suck at plans.

Then it hits me. I have a deal with Luke. I owe him the story of what happened Halloween night. This could be good, it could even be great. Or it could be a total disaster. Good would mean he and BeeBee, and BeeBee and I, all stay friends and Luke and I start planning our first real date. Great would be all of the above but instead of a first date we skip right to planning the honeymoon. Disaster would be losing both of them.

Given my planning skills, which outcome is most likely?

If you said disaster, you win the prize, which is nothing. Be happy, you won't have to pay taxes on it.

I'm not a gambler. I always lose when I gamble.

Then again, losing every bet doesn't mean you're not a gambler. It means you're a lousy gambler, and should probably give it up. I know better than to bet on my favorite team or horse or numbers. Whatever I pick, it's sure to be a loser.

What I am is a risk-taker. I can weigh the odds with the best of them. I don't know who 'them' is, it doesn't matter. I can do the risk vs. reward thing as well as anyone. In this case, I decide it's time to make good on my deal with Luke.

How it impacts my relationship with BeeBee is a bridge I'll cross when I have to.

BeeBee is long gone by the time I pull myself together and face the day. Nice of him to return the favor and let me sleep in.

It's mid-afternoon, time to make a phone call.

The conversation with Luke was strange. Who knows strange better than me? No one. I call, he doesn't answer. Do I leave a voice mail? Hell no. He calls back, but I don't know it's him because it's not his number. Not the one he gave me. I ignore it, and whoever it is leaves a message.

My brain is incapable of seeing the call as anything other than a phone scam. I keep ignoring it until I get a second call from the same number. Another voice mail. Persistent robot-caller, this one. Fine, I'll play.

I have one of those cell phones able to transcribe your voicemail. It allows you to spend your time reading gibberish instead of listening to someone talk for twenty seconds. I hate those transcriptions. I avoid reading them, unless I know who called and don't want to listen to their voice. Then I'll read.

I decide to read this time. The first message is nonsensical to the point it might as well be a foreign language. Thing is, I don't know anyone who speaks such a language. I start to read the second voice mail. It's less mangled than the first and I manage to decipher some of it. I realize it's Luke and switch to the first voicemail and listen, rather than read.

I hear gunshots, wind noise, some shouting, and Luke trying to be heard over it all. Something about shooting (yeah, heard it) and Dawsonville, and 'I'll call you back.' Did the Atlanta PD invade Dawsonville? Why? There's nothing but mountains and outlet malls. I'm a fan of discount shopping, but why are guns involved?

Second voicemail. It's quiet. No wind, no gunshots.

I can hear Luke perfectly when he says, "Hi Charlie, glad you called. Why didn't you leave a message? Is everything OK? I'm in Dawsonville, I brought my son out for some skeet shooting. I'll be home around seven. If you need to talk, call me back. Otherwise, I'll call you when I get home. Glad you called, can't wait to talk. My phone's dead, battery's drained, I can't make calls. This is my son's phone, call me back on this number if you want. Bye."

You're damn right I need to talk. A son? You drop a son on me in a voicemail? I don't like the idea someone else already had Luke's baby. Or is there more than one? Kids are complicated. They're complicated and their presence complicates everything. I need a minute and I take one. Then I call back.

Wherever he went to get out of the wind and away from the shotguns, he's still there.

"Hey Charlie, is everything OK?" He's happy, and yet he seems sincerely concerned. How is it possible? Is this sorcery?

"You have a son?" Why waste time with pleasantries?

"Is there a problem?" Not cheery anymore.

"Does he know you're gay?"

"My son knows all about me. He figured it out right around the time his mother divorced me. Oh yeah, forgot to tell you, I'm divorced. I'm gonna ask you again, is there a problem?"

I can feel the shields go up from 75 miles away.

He went from cheery to intense in a hurry. I suppose I could have been more nuanced in my opening line, but it would have required me to think before I speak.

"No. This is not a problem. Do you have more than one?"

"Why do you ask?"

I know myself. I don't always act like it, but I do. I know I'm asking all the wrong questions. I'm being a jerk. I think my head got out in front of reality. I've been treating this like a fait accompli, a relationship 'done deal,' when he's living in the real world. I'm some guy he's interested in, no more. This realization is comforting, I manage to relax.

"You sound upset."

"Answer the question Charlie, or I'm hanging up."

"We're all onions, the best way to peel back the layers is to ask the questions."

"This is not the time," he says and I know he's right.

"For what it's worth Luke, your revelation makes you more interesting to me. I like your layers. I want to keep peeling." Yes, I did say those words. Amazing anyone buys my books.

He starts laughing his amazing deep full-throated laugh of his, and I listen because who knows how many times I'll get to hear it again.

"Damn, Charlie, you are one odd duck. No wonder I can't stop thinkin' about you."

What? Did I hear him correctly? Why yes, Mr. Barnes, you did. I'm expecting a hard 'no' when I ask, "Are you free tonight?"

"Sure. How 'bout I swing by after I drop Jason at his mom's? I can grab dinner for us, or we can see what Brian dropped off and make din-din."

He said 'din-din.' Is it cute? I'm not sure. I don't like it.

"Sounds great."

"I'll see you at 7:30, give or take."

"Perfect. See you then."

"Hey Charlie, before I go… is this when you make good on our arrangement?"

This question makes me happy. It saves me the trouble of bringing it up.

"It's the minimum I plan to do tonight."

"Can't wait. See you later."

"Bye," but he's already hung up.

Strange was the wrong word to describe the conversation. No, strange was exactly the right word, but not bad-strange. This was a rare variety of good-strange.

***

It was more like 8:00 p.m. when he showed up. I'm a night owl, eating dinner after 8:00 p.m. is not unusual for me. In fact, skipping dinner entirely is the norm for me. What's unusual is not having a drink at 5:00. Or 6:00. Or 7:00. At 7:55 when I decided he wasn't going to show up at all, I made myself a nice martini to drown my impending sorrow.

I had the glass to my lips, about to take my first sip, when he walked in. Didn't knock, the door was unlocked, he bounced right in. I was rewatching an amazing Kathy Griffin special, 'A Hell of a Story.' It's the one where this twat Andy pretends he doesn't know Kathy after the fake controversy about her and a fake severed head.

In other words, I didn't hear him.

His timing sucked. He startled me and I spilled my drink. On top of wasting perfectly good vodka, I was wearing it all over my face and shirt. I stand up and try to wipe my face.

"You started without me," he pretends to be offended.

"No, asshole, I've been waiting for hours. And I'm bathing in vodka instead of drinking it."

"Is there more?"

"Of course, where do you think you are?"

He kisses me, not full on the lips, as they say, but a nice smooch on the cheek. He slaps my ass and says, "Atta boy, make me a drink, I'll get started on dinner."

'Atta boy?' Who says Atta boy? Is this what giddy feels like? Like a teenager finding out their crush has a crush on them too. How cute. I think I might like being bossed around by Luke. Not bossed around, more like directed. Is this making sense? Who knows. I'm goin' with it.

"You got it boss. Olives?" I've never spoken like this before.

"Dealer's choice," He shouts to me from the kitchen.

Something tells me he's the dealer. I can live with it. I've shuffled and I've dealt. Multi-talented, I am.

I hear him opening cabinets, placing things on the counter, getting out pots or pans, or some such things. I don't cook, I don't know how to use most of the crap in the kitchen. BeeBee gave me a list, I gave the list to a salesperson at Macy's. Instant kitchen.

I make his drink, slam what's left of mine, and make another for myself. I decide olives are the right way to go. I put the drinks down and say, "I gotta change my shirt, your drink is on the table, two olives for you."

He doesn't respond. Odd, but okay, he's focused. There's this rustling sound. I don't know how to describe it. Something makes a muffled thump on the floor in the kitchen. I don't give it more thought as I head to my bedroom. I'm in my closet, peeling off my shirt when I suddenly feel like I'm being watched. Because I am being watched. Not exactly super-power stuff.

Luke is standing there, wearing nothing but my ugly green and orange apron, holding our drinks, with a smile that put every last tooth in his head on display. He has nice teeth, I'm sure they cost his parents a bundle.

"I take it dinner's gonna be delayed."

He holds out my drink and commands, "Leave your shirt off, join me in the kitchen."

I take the drink and he turns around to go back to the kitchen. I have to move quickly to keep my eyes on those amazing round mounds moving away from me. Yes, this is wild and probably not hygienic, but what the hell, I'm all in. I pinch myself. This is becoming a habit, making sure I'm awake. If I've fallen asleep on the sofa and this is a dream, I want to wake up before it goes too far. Nope, it hurt, this is real.

We had a pretty normal evening, all things considered. He cooked, I stared at his ass, we chatted, I made more drinks. The highlights: Jason is 13 and his only child, Luke and his ex-wife agreed to be friendly and co-parent, he spends at least two weekends a month with his son, and their favorite pastimes are hunting, fishing, and Atlanta United football games. And Luke is off on Mondays. Which is tomorrow.

He's off tomorrow. Could this night get any better? Why yes, it can.

We eat, still chatting about his life, his kid, his burgeoning friendship with Brian Barkin. His word, burgeoning, I wouldn't use it. What's the point? Too hard to spell.

Through all of this, all he had on was my ugly yet beautifully tight apron, and I was shirtless. By the time dinner was over, it felt perfectly natural. In retrospect, I think it was the point of the exercise. An exercise in making one's intentions clear. Luke, he is clever. Which is why, when I asked if he wanted to hear my story, the one he came to hear, I was not the least bit surprised when he asked, "How 'bout we talk about it over breakfast?"

"What are you making?"

To which he smiled his toothy smile, leaned in close and said, "Who cares? Let's go to bed."

And we did. And it was great. Not amazing, my ribs hurt like hell and I had to be careful about where I put my face for fear of hitting my still-healing nose. Admittedly, it makes it sound less than great. I'll say this, the night gave me a taste of what was possible. And what I was likely to ruin by the time we finished breakfast.

I enjoyed every second of it, the pleasure and the pain. There was the added bonus of knowing whatever was happening between Luke and BeeBee, it wasn't this.

***

I said I wouldn't give details. Get over yourself. Details are private. I already said more than I should. Not porn, not erotica. If you don't like it, go watch a movie.

Coffee, the one thing I know how to make. BeeBee taught me. It was a requirement. Can't make coffee, can't be friends. I never knew how much better coffee smelled in the morning when the person you spent the night with wakes up and brews a fresh pot. Luke got up before me. Remember, I don't do early. I woke up some time before 9:00 a.m. and, were it not for the smell of coffee and bacon, I might have killed someone. There's no reason to be up before 10.

Not Luke, I wouldn't kill my naked chef. I'd find some random person on the street to vent my rage on.

OK, no, I wouldn't.

Coffee. Bacon. My home smells better than the Golden Skillet.

The Golden Skillet is this semi-famous greasy spoon diner on 14th street. I don't know why people call it a greasy spoon, I've never once had a dirty utensil there, and I've been a patron for years. Greasy spoon, I guess it's an alternate term for 'local diner.' Or it's a way to manage expectations. Whatever, it works. The place is old-school; production companies rent it out to shoot movies and TV episodes inside. I love the Golden Skillet. A ride-share from my place costs about five bucks, before tip. Weekends are best, the place fills with college kids and people trying to hang on to their youth, nursing hangovers with hot greasy food and coffee strong enough you can eat with a fork.

BeeBee and I are on a first name basis with every employee.

Luke is in my kitchen doing his best to recreate the ambience, or at least the smell, of the Golden Skillet. He's exceeding his mandate, for certain. I sit up in bed. I consider waltzing into my kitchen naked and decide against it. As I'm pondering this monumental choice, Luke walks in wearing his underwear, and says, "Hit the shower Charlie, breakfast in ten."

Then he walks out. He's a boxer briefs guy, like me. It's impossible to refuse a directive from a well-built, handsome man wearing them. They have special powers.

Quick shower, throw on some shorts and a sweatshirt, and I'm in the kitchen.

"You're overdressed," he says, and he's serious about it. He doesn't smile when he says it. What have I gotten myself into with this one? Naturally, I strip down to my undies.

"Much better."

"I aim to please."

"So far, so good."

He has Jedi mind powers I can't resist.

"Grab your coffee and take a seat, I'll bring you a plate."

I do as I'm told. For the sake of my future as a human being, I cannot allow anyone to know about this. If Dez finds out I'm capable of following instructions, I'll never hear the end of it. It would completely shift the nature of our relationship.

I pour. I sit. He brings us each a plate. He sits. We are there, at my dining table, about to eat breakfast, in our underwear. I have travelled through a black hole and arrived at an alternate reality. I think I like it. Forget hygiene, let's eat.

"Last night was fun," he says.

Fun? Is he making small talk, fishing for a compliment, or about to tell me I need to up my game in the bedroom? It better not be the latter. Has he forgotten I recently got out of the hospital? How could he? My face is still purple, in places starting to turn yellow, and my ribs look like they were stepped on by an elephant. I'm grateful my lip is fully healed. Would have been awkward. And gross. Enough.

Elephants, I mean no disrespect, I doubt one would ever intentionally step on a human. I like elephants. Ask me why someday.

"Fun? It was more than fun to me." I respond this way because I want him to get to the point.

"I did most of the work," he says, but smiles when he says it.

This is good.

"We should have waited until I wasn't covered in bruises."

Here he catches me by surprise, "I think your bruises are sexy."

I don't miss a beat, "What happens when they're gone?"

"We can make some news one," he says, without the hint of an expression on his face.

No way, not gonna do it. This is no Fifty Shades of anything. Then his face breaks apart. He starts laughing at me. I must have let out some audible sigh of relief.

"The look on your face…"

I can't help it, I laugh with him.

"I always say a little pain goes a long way. I think we hit my limit last night."

"I think you have more in you."

Breakfast is light. One strip of bacon, one scrambled egg, half an English muffin. It takes about two minutes to eat. We abandon our coffee.

Rinse and repeat, it's noon before we get around to having an actual conversation. I don't mind the delay.

I will say this, take it how you will, having sex when your house smells like a diner is distracting. It took me about 20 seconds to get over it.

CHAPTER SEVEN

Kryptonite

I fell asleep. I never fall asleep after sex, not during the day. When I wake up, I check the time, 11:45 a.m. Time for lunch. Luke is not in bed. I hear the shower and realize he dozed off too. The water cuts off and I hear wet footsteps heading toward the bedroom.

My place is old, it predates the concept of 'en suite' bathrooms. Mine is down the hall. I hate this, but in this situation, it gives me a distinct feeling of anticipation, listening to his wet feet slapping their way toward me. He steps into the room, still dripping wet, casually drying off with what I think is my last clean towel.

I think I should describe Luke. I've mentioned parts, blue eyes, handsome face, perfect ass. It's time for more detail. Luke is a bit shorter than me. I'm six-one, which makes him five-eleven. Note about me worth mentioning, I've never dated anyone taller than me. Had sex with, yes. Dated, never. There was the time my roommate and I hooked up a few (several) times during his last month living with me. He was gorgeous, I had to make an exception. But we weren't dating. Had he stuck around even a few weeks longer, who knows, the exception might have become the rule. We'll never know. Having sex while living together does not necessarily constitute dating, no matter how much you like someone. It's in the rule book, look it up.

Back to Luke.

Five-eleven. Athletic build. Beefy chest, shoulders, arms. Thick legs too. Word to all you gym rats, do not skip leg days. Skinny legs are red flag. Skinny legs with big arms mean you are a vain lazy dimwit. Work those pathetic calves and thighs, or give it up entirely.

Luke has worked every muscle in his body, it's obvious. He looks like a college wrestler, without the cauliflower ears. What sets off his build is his chest hair.

I cannot grow chest hair. Way back in my family tree, an ancestor married an Indigenous person (this is no lie, I can prove it, piss off if you don't believe me). There is nothing indigenous about me, I'm not making any claims beyond this one. What came down to me over the intervening generations was an inability to grow chest hair, or much hair on any part of my body. I have peach-fuzzy legs and peach-fuzzy arms, nothing more beyond the expected, you know, locations.

Some guys spend a fortune to get the hairless look I get by way of genetics. Go ahead, be jealous.

Luke has perfect body hair. Swirling eddies of silky black hair on his pecks, spinning 'round to form a line between his abs, flowing gracefully like a river through an Alpine valley, right down to his manicured garden of earthly delights. He manscapes. Attractive and practical. Nice. Dark hair, beefy body, piercing blue eyes, and the world's best body hair.

I am opposite. Guys tell me I'm good looking. I don't know. I'm vain, and I don't think I'll ever live up to my own expectations. Enough about me, this isn't therapy.

Luke is precisely the physical build to which I am most physically attracted. But his personality is turning out to be his secret weapon, and my kryptonite. Different from anyone I've ever met, at least in how I respond to him.

Which is why, as he's standing there toweling off and dripping all over my floor, I can't do anything but smile and stare at him. For a minute he stands there and smiles back. The spell is broken when he tosses the towel at me, says, "You're up, champ," and walks into my closet. I'm thinking, yes, something in there will fit him as he says, "Hope you don't mind sharing."

Before I can respond, because, what the hell am I going to say, he's in the doorway of my closet, slipping on a pair of my gym shorts. He's going commando. I guess it's ok to share a wet towel but he draws the line at fresh undies?

"Might be cold in those." I'm being serious. It's November. It does get cold here in November, sometimes.

He turns back into the closet, grabs a t-shirt. One of my favorites, plain back V-neck, loose on me but tight on him. I decide he can keep it. As long as he wears it in my presence.

"I take it we're staying in?" I ask this even though it's obvious.

"Damn strait. Time to make good on our deal Charlie. Fun time is over."

His euphemism for sex is 'fun.' I can go with it. He walks out, down the hall, and I hear the TV turn on. The cable is working again, hurray. He puts it on MSNBC. My feelings are completely mixed. I'm confused, and disappointed, by his change in tone, wondering what exactly he's up to, with regard to me. On the other hand, I'm grateful to all the powers of the universe, this and any others, he does not watch Fox News. Total deal breaker.

I take my time in the shower. I'm not avoiding the inevitable, I'm enjoying a nice hot shower. No, I'm avoiding. This is not going to be easy. I will tell him what I did, why I did it, and how it landed me in the hospital.

While I'm running up my gas bill, I think about the possible outcomes. He might find it funny and let it go. I'm not optimistic enough to think this will happen. I'm not dumb enough to hope for it.

On to the next. He could get pissed off and walk out, never to be seen again. This one is pretty high on the probability scale, but not the worst outcome.

He could decide to arrest me. He made a promise, a pinky swear, and I assume he's a man of his word. I don't have any reason to assume, other than I want it to be true. And, the fact he's exceeded my expectations on every other front. I suppose it makes him an overachiever.

He could take what I tell him and hand it over to one of his detective buddies. They could then arrest some people, including me. Then Luke never speaks to me again. As I consider this possibility, I get an intense shiver.

I've run out of hot water.

The last possibility scares me. I'm not easily scared, but this has implications far beyond me and my lust for Luke. I don't know why, but as I'm standing there toweling off with a damp towel, thinking about how I'm disgusted with the idea of sharing a towel, I feel an intense sense of calm wash over me.

I relax. I realize I'm being ridiculous. It's ridiculous for me to give a rat's ass about how he reacts. What's done is done and whatever comes next, I'll deal with it. I mean, I like the guy, but I still don't know him. Found out yesterday he has a kid. Recently saw him naked for the first time. The list of firsts goes on and gets better, but I've made my point. I have this figured out.

I'm deliberate about the clothes I put on. Keep it casual, but warm enough I won't have to change if a SWAT team crashes through my door and hauls me away. I know, it's silly. But it's better to prepared. Jeans, a t-shirt, a sweatshirt, and no, I am not going commando. In jeans, are you crazy? All the chafing. A thick pair of socks, and I'm ready to go.

I decide I'm going to keep it light, try to make him laugh. Instead of walking down the hall, I build up some speed and try to slide into view on the hardwood floor, à la Risky Business, but fully clothed. This maneuver does not go as planned.

When I bought my place, and my book sales cratered, I had to scrap most of my renovation plans. One thing I didn't scrap? Refinishing the floors. The child in me, which is most of what's in me, loves to slide around in my socks on these amazing, shiny, smooth, wide-plank floors. Knotty pine, gorgeous.

I run down the hall, it's a long hall, twist myself sideways to slide into view, trying to stop right in the middle of the wide arch between the hall and the living room.

Instead, I slide into view, shout 'tah-dah' like I'm modern-day vaudevillian. The moment he looks up at me and starts to smile, I slide right by past the arch and slam into the front door, which makes a loud cracking sound but doesn't break. I bounce off the door and land with a nice smack on those shiny wide planks. Yes, it hurts more than my pride.

I'm sure it was much funnier than it sounds. It must have been, because as I was trying to catch my breath and pick myself up off the floor, all I could hear over my heavy breathing was Luke's laughter. Poor execution, but I got the result I wanted, I'll call it a win.

Ever the chivalrous sort, Luke, still laughing, pries himself off the sofa and comes to my aid. He helps me up for the second time in my life, and through his laughter he asks me, "Buddy, what are you doin'? Are you okay?"

Here's where you might be thinking, 'Buddy? You had sex with this guy twice in less than twenty-four hours, and he calls you buddy? What type of buddy does that make you?'

I was thinking the same. Then I remember, this is a guy who likes shooting shotguns at clay ashtrays. He probably calls everyone 'buddy.' He probably calls his dog 'buddy.' Does he have a dog? I should ask.

He sees I'm in pain and doesn't stop laughing until I'm plunked down on the sofa. It makes me like him even more. I'd rather not see pity in his eyes, or have him act concerned. I don't need any of it. I need a beer. Too early, though day drinking is a temporary salve for many wounds.

Why is it, if you have a beer over lunch on Saturday, it's fine, but if you have beer at noon on a Monday, you're a drunk. Another one of life's mysteries.

He fetches me a cold bottle of water, where did it come from? I have bottled water? I guess I do. BeeBee was right, I need to open my fridge more often. I can't remember the last time I bought groceries. I wonder how long BeeBee has been doing this for me? One day I will be an adult and manage my own provisioning. Or not. Who knows with me?

I'm thinking all these deep thoughts when I realize Luke is sitting on the sofa staring at me. Not looking at me, staring at me. And not smiling.

"What? Haven't you ever seen a guy fall on his ass before?" I say, with healthy dose of bitchiness.

"Your lips move when you think," he replies.

I spend too much time alone.

He follows his observation with, "You're blushing."

He's smiling again. Oh, kill me, please, I'm never going to get anything right again in my life, why try?

"Don't be embarrassed, it's cute. Jason does it too."

He's comparing me to his son. Is this a one-off, or have we stumbled onto something deeper in his psyche? I do not have daddy issues. Do not go there.

"It's OK, people do it when they're thinking and stop paying attention to their environment. Everyone does it, but usually not in front of other people."

"You mean like masturbation?" I ask. This is intriguing. It might also keep him from mentioning his son again.

"I'm not sure it's the comparison I would make, but sure, like masturbation."

"Are you analyzing me or something?" I ask. I think I'm onto him.

"Can't help it. Comes with the job. What were you thinking about?"

You don't read lips too? I wonder this, but don't ask because I don't want to know.

"It's a useful tool in my field. I can't read minds, but lips I can usually manage."

Can't read minds? I beg to differ. Let's test his powers. "What do you think I was I thinking?"

"I don't know. Something about Brian, 'BeeBee' causes a distinct lip movement pattern. But your lips didn't move much before you tuned back into me. It's all I got."

"Easy guess, I'm always thinking about BeeBee, for one reason or another."

"You love him, don't you?"

"Of course, he's my best friend. We're family," I say, and I mean it, and he better not question it.

"Did you ever have sex with him?"

At first, I'm angry he asked, then curious. Then back to angry. I realize Luke is staring at me again. My lips were not moving, I was all feeling and no thought. He's up to something. "It's a personal question. Why do you ask?"

"I want to know where I stand, with both of you."

My anger subsides. Still, this feels like a manipulation. I know manipulation well. It's been said of me, by me, I'm not nice, I'm manipulative. Because I'm good at it. Manipulation works. Live by the sword, blah, blah, blah.

"Yes, and before you ask, it was in college, it was his first time, and I'm not sure, but I think it was good we got it out of the way then, because it set us up for the relationship we have. Satisfied detective?"

"Thank you for being honest with me Charlie."

I'm right. This is a manipulation. Bad liars and poker players have at least one thing in common. A 'tell.'

A 'tell' is a facial tick, an eye movement, a change in skin color, pupil dilation, a head movement, which gives away the fact a person is lying, or a poker player is bluffing. Why do you think professional poker players wear sunglasses at the table?

In the last few minutes, Luke has seen me embarrassed, angry, and completely honest. He's looking for my tell.

What he doesn't know is I know exactly what my tell is. I'm not telling what my tell is, because then everyone would be able to tell when I'm lying. Knowing what it is, I have a fighting chance of controlling it. Luke's manipulation goes deeper. He knows I love BeeBee. And I have no reason to lie about it. He probably already knew I'd had sex with BeeBee. BeeBee told Luke his real name. Revealing a sexual past with me is small potatoes by comparison. No, it's not a euphemism for testicles. Not this time anyway.

His first question was a control question, and the second question a test. I know this because I had to pass a polygraph, a lie detector test, when a bunch of crap went missing from a store I worked at when I was in high school. I didn't steal a thing, and I quit my job exactly one second after they told me I 'passed.' I knew I passed. I also read everything I could about polygraph tests before I ever sat down for theirs. Those things are useless, which is why you can't use them in court. Turns out, one of the owners' kids, who didn't have to take the test, was the actual thief. Too bad you can't fire your kids. Dammit my lips are moving.

"You're welcome. Any more questions on this topic, or can

we move on?" I'm not afraid to be annoyed.

I'm not surprised when he says "One more."

"Let's have it."

"You love him," he says.

Is he not listening?

"Yes, we've established this detail. Next?"

Then he knocks me into another place entirely when he says, "And you took a beating for him because of it."

We are definitely not in Kansas anymore.

"How did we go from screwing like bunnies to a full-on interrogation in under an hour?"

I know I made a deal but this is a bit much.

"The day's not gettin' any younger Charlie. I thought you would appreciate the direct approach."

I'm starting to not care what happens next.

"If you want to be direct, why not spell it out?"

"I don't understand the question," he says, and no way do I believe he's the least bit confused.

"Clearly you have your own idea about what happened. Spare us both the drama and lay it out. I'll let you know what you've got right, and what you don't."

"Not our agreement. I want to hear it from you. The mule's mouth."

Hint, hint. He gave me a hint. If he's willing to butcher a cliche to drop a hint, then I think he knows a lot. Good. This might be easier than expected. As in, everything I say will be the truth, as will everything I don't say. Fun time is indeed over. I'm annoyed and he's professional. This is work for him. Or has it been work all along?

"What type of detective are you?"

"Narcotics."

By the way he says it, with a note of surprise, he seems to think I should know this already. I never gave it a thought before. Why would I? I assumed he was naturally curious, about me. I can be extremely obtuse at times.

The conversation was more of a monologue, punctuated by narrow, focused, questions. Luke barely made a comment on any of it. He also didn't take a single note. I kept thinking 'Is he recording this?'

In a nutshell, I told him I'd been hauling drugs cross country for the last eighteen months, give or take a year. I lose track of time. If you don't believe me, ask my publisher. Don't judge. Or, go ahead and judge, then piss off.

My last trip didn't go as planned. I've said many times I'm terrible at planning, but the last trip wasn't my plan. I got caught. Bad, but not the bad news. Let's start at the beginning. The bad news won't make sense without it. I think there's more bad news to follow, stay with me.

It started out innocent enough, then things went about as sideways as they could go. But I'm jumping ahead.

In the state of Georgia, at the time I started my side hustle, medical marijuana was barely legal, and the list of ailments for which it could be prescribed was woefully short. Plus, there was limited supply. In other words, medical marijuana in Georgia was bullshit. The people who could benefit from it couldn't get it, and if even they could, their eligibility was based on a short list of medical conditions. If you happened to be one of the lucky few who qualified, all you could get was 'low THC oil', twenty ounces or less at any given time. Anyone who uses pot for pain knows this oil is crap. If you're a cancer patient who needs THC for nausea from chemo, it's even less than crap.

I had cancer. Not recently. Long before pot, of any kind, was legal anywhere. The chemo was brutal. A friend hooked me up with a bong and some bud and next thing you know, no more nausea. I could eat again. I stopped losing weight. Eighty-five pounds in three months is like losing a whole person. Granted, the person would be tiny, like Prince or

Johnny Weir, but it's a lot.

This was high risk for me, for reasons way beyond legal. The cancer had spread to my lungs. Breathing was difficult; smoking was a chore. The bong made all the difference. I will never take my lungs for granted again. This is where I answer the inevitable question 'Which cancer did you have?'

The one that kills you, thanks for asking. I used to answer the same way every time I got the question. Then I decided, to hell with it, they asked, I'm gonna answer.

I had metastatic testicular cancer. My testicles were trying to kill me. More precisely, my left testicle. The right one was happy as it was, hanging out and doing its factory work. But the left one, the monster got as big as a tennis ball before they took it out. If a giant testicle sounds like fun to you, I suggest you stuff a tennis ball in your briefs and carry it around for a few weeks, then tell me how you feel.

Cancer isn't funny, but talking about it can lead to some funny comments, and surviving it can forever alter your sense of humor. It's easier when it's behind you, and you didn't die. Luke interrupted this part of my monologue with his insight "Geez, Charlie, I wondered what was going on down there. I thought you had small balls."

I found this funny, but he felt bad. Not because of the 'small balls' comment, it was a joke. Making a joke of it is why he felt bad. It's complicated. I ended up dropping my drawers and walking him through the entire anatomical structure and surgical process. He was impressed they took the tennis ball out through my lower abdomen, the scar bears witness to the size of the thing.

I'd never done this before, no one ever had the balls to ask for this level of detail. Yes, it's a bad pun. Accept it, and love me for my flaws. We had this refreshingly matter-of-fact, clinical conversation about it.

"Interesting, I'm glad you're okay, but what's it got to do

with anything?" he asks while I pulled my jeans up.

Back to business.

I explained how BeeBee had a friend who was getting chemo, and their anti- nausea meds weren't getting the job done. BeeBee knows all about my missing piece, he rode the entire ordeal out with me, and he asked if I could help out. BeeBee's friend used to have connections in the ATL, but not anymore.

I could not help. I had no idea how to buy pot. Like many things in my life, the process had been handled by someone else. After I recovered, the process ended. And yet, I know what it's like to be chemo-sick. I gave it some thought. Truth is, I gave it lots of thought. I figured it out. Turns out, it was easy. Expensive, but easy.

All I had to do was go where recreational pot was legal, and purchase restrictions weren't too tight, buy the right edibles, and get them back to Atlanta. I'm not giving up all the details. Luke was shocked by the simplicity, until he remembered it was my plan, it had to be simple.

I'm a points whore. Airline points, hotel points, online shopping points. I love points, they're quite rewarding. On my first trip to Potlandia, a cross-country flight, I flew first class. If a flight is over sixty minutes in duration, I'm flying first class, or I'm not going. Period. End of discussion. I had points for my first trip. I stayed in a five-star hotel for one night, on points. Rented a big-ass SUV, with points. Luxury travel, zero dollars.

I came back with enough edibles to last one person six months, which was more than BeeBee's friend, let's call him Harvey, needed. Of course, when you're a cancer patient going through chemotherapy, you meet other cancer patients going through chemotherapy.

It's like having a kid who plays soccer. You meet other people who have kids who play soccer. It might be the one thing you have in common, but you have it, and it's enough for you to develop a connection, enough for you to talk about soccer. Soccer equipment, soccer coaches, soccer games.

Cancer patients don't talk to each other much when they're getting chemo, but it does happen. Especially when one of them is high. Harvey was high when he started chatting up a fellow soccer mom and mentioned how much better he was feeling since he started getting high. He could eat again, what a miracle. You see where this is going.

He shared. Too much.

Then he needed more edibles. As did his friend, and her two friends, and it went on from there. Turns out, a lot of people have cancer with poorly managed chemo side-effects. Next thing you know, I'm hauling pot edibles across the country, supplying them to cancer patients across the Atlanta metro area, through Harvey. In return, I'm spending quality time in a beautiful part of the country at minimal cost, if you ignore the inherent risk I was taking, which I rated as low.

I would give Harvey the receipts and he would reimburse me. But points don't last forever and once they ran out, one paid trip in first class and overnight fancy-pants accommodations caused a loud sucking sound to emanate from my bank account. I told Harvey it was my last trip.

This is where BeeBee re-enters the story. Since BeeBee manages my money, what there is of it, he knew I wouldn't be flying coach or sleeping in a cheap motel. He came up with an alternate plan. His plan got me caught. His plan got my ass kicked.

My ass, not his.

CHAPTER EIGHT

About a BeeBee

One of the things BeeBee grew to hate about working as a prosecutor was prosecuting people. Not everyone deserves to go to jail for the crimes they commit. A lot of people go to jail because they can't afford an attorney, and public defenders are burned out, overworked, and trying to make it to the weekend. Deals are made. Agree to this, get something in return. No need for a trial.

There are people in jail for years on end who should never have gone to jail in the first place. It is the single most idiotic aspect about our justice system. I'll climb off the soapbox, but I may come back to this later. Consider yourself warned.

BeeBee grew to hate it. He also started to hate politics. Hated his job, hated one of the primary career paths out of it. But he didn't drop everything one day in a fit of rage. He's too smart.

His mother died.

About BeeBee's mother. I met her twice. Once when she came to our college for a visit, and once when I went to St. Thomas with BeeBee. We were there for ten days. She was beautiful, in every describable way, and in a bunch of ways I can't describe. Whatever I say won't do her justice. Suffice it to say, after a few days with her, I felt like she had adopted me. I don't know everything BeeBee told her about me, but she welcomed me like a prodigal son.

She sang in the best clubs in the best resorts all over the Caribbean. She would take a small plane, occasionally a boat, to work three or four days a week, often spending an extra night or two, once BeeBee was old enough to be on his own. She loved it, and she was great at it.

Cruise ships have these people called Cruise Directors. The bigger the ship, the more Cruise Directors onboard. Every Cruise Director on every cruise ship in the Caribbean knew about BeeBee's mother. She was the Caribbean's answer to Francine Reed. If you don't know about Francine Reed, you know nothing about music.

Her name was Bessie. Bessie Barkin. Her stage name was Bessie Lester. She never sought fame, but her talent made her a small fortune. Bessie was a saver, a passion she passed on to BeeBee. When she died, she left it all to BeeBee. She owned her house outright, BeeBee still owns it. Bessie and BeeBee's father never married. He didn't want to leave his wife back in Houston, and Bessie was at peace with the situation.

Yeah, he was a lousy husband, but he was a decent father to BeeBee, when he was there.

He didn't challenge Bessie's will. He offered to add to it, wanted to give BeeBee the money from their joint account in St. Thomas. Hell yes, BeeBee accepted, but it spawned a new problem. More taxes.

BeeBee's mother worked her ass off for her money, it doesn't matter she enjoyed her work. BeeBee was outraged by the taxes he paid. He decided to become an estate attorney, and learn how to help other people avoid the same fate. He never does anything half-assed, like me. No way. He threw himself into it, before he quit his day job. Once he had all the training, landed a couple of clients, and felt he was good at it, he left the prosecutor's office. Walked out without ever looking back.

Until Harvey and his cohort of cancer patients needed more than I could provide. This part piqued Luke's interest. The part he'd been waiting for. The part where I realized I should have left BeeBee out of the entire story.

One of the things BeeBee did after he quit his job and struck out on his own was to try to make things right for some of the people he put away. Look, the system is the system. Until you change the system, this will keep happening. BeeBee wanted to help, or he wanted to make amends. Does it matter which? Not in my book.

As a result, BeeBee developed friendships, real friendships, nothing like mine and his of course, with some of the same people he prosecuted. He set up a non-profit, got other attorneys to work with him, usually pro bono, and set about getting people out of jail. It was hard work, but he cared. He leaned into the challenge.

It garnered him enemies to balance out the new friends. A former prosecutor un-prosecuting people, it wasn't a great look and BeeBee was a thorn in more than a few sides.

This is the honest-to-whatever-you-pray-to truth, BeeBee did not know the extent of my activities. Because I didn't tell him, especially when I lost control of the whole enchilada. Before it happened, BeeBee noticed I spent well beyond my allowance one month, which could leave me short of cash at tax time, which was fast approaching. As a writer, a self-employed person, I'm told my taxes are more complicated than, say, a marketing manager or a fast-food employee. And yes, BeeBee, my genius friend, 'allows' me to spend a certain amount of money each month. Don't knock it, it works, most of the time. He also handles my taxes. Not sure who does them, but BeeBee makes sure they get done. Once the travel expenses started stacking up, he started asking questions. Yes, I lied to him and said they were for research or my new book. He believed me, then suggested I turn myself into a business. An LLC, to be precise. A 'limited liability company,' something I'd heard of but knew nothing about.

It's cool. It's like a corporation and a sole proprietorship got together and had a baby. A baby with no legal liability for the debts, or other entanglements, of the baby, the company. Yes, it's an oversimplified and potentially inaccurate description, but nobody's here for my business acumen.

It meant my travel expenses could become business expenses, and I could take on partners, and their money. In my mind, we were forming a charitable enterprise to help me carry on the good work on behalf of Harvey and the seemingly ever-growing list of patients who needed us.

If you're reading this and the idea scares you, it should. Luke's reaction to this part of my story was the first hint of real trouble. He was way happier than I expected. I thought this part would bore him. Nope, he was thrilled, asked lots of questions.

Which worried me.

I felt compelled to explain, over and over, BeeBee did not set up the LLC and he did not provide any money. You can do anything online, including setting up an LLC. I felt compelled because Luke kept asking me if BeeBee did any of these things. Every time I answered, Luke stared at me with his lie detector eyes and listened as if his life depended on ingesting and dissecting every single word. Repeatedly.

BeeBee was trying to do something nice. He was trying to give back. I was trying to rack up huge points and take nice trips across the country without going broke. I had started staying for a few days at a time, to have some fun. And it was fun. I saw no reason to stop, as long I could afford to keep going. It was a true win-win. I was having fun, cancer patients were eating well, nobody was getting hurt, and I had a way to avoid going broke.

Writers are all this way, we love experience. Most writers draw their best material from personal experience. I'm no exception. The difference is, my life experience before this was a lot less fun. I wonder if all this activity impacted the quality of my second book? We may never know.

I formed an LLC. With Harvey. Online, it was easy.

Harvey was one of the people BeeBee got out of jail, after having put him there in the first place. To my knowledge, Harvey was not a bad guy, at least as far as I knew when I met him. Long before I met him, he got pulled over. He wasn't stoned, wasn't drunk, wasn't even speeding. He had a busted taillight. He also had about 28 grams of ambrosial (if you like skunk) pot in his center console.

The weight is important. It's an ounce of pot. At the time, an ounce of pot, in Georgia, was a felony. It's enough to get you ten years if you don't have a good attorney. BeeBee was the prosecuting attorney. When a prosecuting attorney is presented with evidence, he or she tends to accept certain aspects of the evidence at face value. Like the weight of seized drugs. A prosecutor doesn't keep a scale around to weigh the evidence. They trust this detail is fact derived from good police work, not a made up or falsified number.

Harvey got a court appointed attorney who came to BeeBee with a deal. Drop the 'intent to distribute' charge and go with simple possession, and Harvey would plead guilty.

Harvey had rolled up all his pot into nice, tight joints, ready for smoking.

You might think this clearly demonstrates an intent to distribute. It's exactly what BeeBee was thinking, but he made the deal. Why wouldn't he? The sentencing range is the same either way, and Harvey's attorney offered it up. Apparently, she was hoping for some mercy from the court.

Mercy? In Atlanta? She must have been high herself. Harvey got nine years. They took one off, since he spent a year in jail waiting to go to trial.

Single most idiotic aspect of our system. Worth repeating.

This conviction was one of BeeBee's last before his mother passed away. And one of the first he revisited. BeeBee knew what a lot of people don't. In some cases, evidence is kept until the convicted person's sentence is complete. This was one of those cases. When BeeBee mentioned this to a young attorney working on the case, she got the crazy idea to weigh the evidence. Literally, put the shit on a scale and see what you get.

Twenty-one grams. Simple possession. It took three months, but Harvey was released for time served. He did three years. The standard sentence for simple possession is twelve months or less. He should have been released as soon as he entered his guilty plea. BeeBee helped him find a couple more attorneys, and before it was all over, Harvey had a settlement.

It was a painful lesson for BeeBee. He trusted the accuracy of the evidence presented. It cost Harvey over two years of his life, cost the state a chunk of cash, and nearly ruined BeeBee's faith in humanity. Oddly enough, it also restored it. Because Harvey never blamed BeeBee. He wasn't angry or vengeful. He expressed gratitude things turned his way, and made a personal commitment to walk the straight and narrow path for the rest of his life.

At first, no one would hire Harvey for any meaningful work. Instead, he used his settlement to go to school. He became an accountant. A CPA. He found work, had great benefits, got married, and eventually went to work for himself. Then he was diagnosed with cancer. Pancreatic cancer. The one-year survival rate, twenty percent. The five-year survival rate, about seven percent.

The first person he called, after telling his wife, was BeeBee. He didn't ask for anything, wanted BeeBee to know. Less than a year into his treatment, because Harvey was not giving up, odds be damned, he divorced his wife. Because of BeeBee, Harvey had a prenup. And yet, she took a pile of his assets as parting gifts. Harvey started losing clients and next thing you know, he's approaching hard times again.

I didn't know all of this when I first met Harvey. I knew some of it, but not all of it. From my perspective, he was BeeBee's friend and he needed some help with his chemo side effects, and I was the person BeeBee knew who had relevant experience.

Knowing more about Harvey may have changed my mind about helping him. Probably would have changed my mind about setting up our 'business,' and most definitely would have prepared me for what Luke had to say about Harvey.

But we're not there yet. I still have more explaining to do.

Like how I got caught, and what came after.

The butterfly effect. One seemingly small incident can have a huge impact on some later event. It's from chaos theory, which one could argue is the driving force of my life. Chaos.

I formed an LLC, with Harvey as a partner. He put money in, and would cover travel expenses, up to a point. Even if I had known more about Harvey's personal life, I probably wouldn't have put two and two together because, well, it's math. Math is hard, I'd rather go dancing.

I don't like to dance. As BeeBee liked to say, "you got rhythm, but you got no moves." I like to go, because it's fun to watch, and if it's late enough everybody's drunk or high and the lights are low and my lack of moves goes unnoticed.

I also lack an eye for the big picture. Two years, give or take a year, into my arrangement with Harvey, he decided on a new strategy.

A month after I said I wasn't taking any more trips, Harvey

comes up with a more 'efficient and streamlined' plan. It made perfect sense to me, because I'm an idiot.

Harvey's new plan was simple enough. Up the ante, shorten the trip. I'll go for the day, with ten grand on hand instead of the usual thousand bucks. He gives me a map of all the stops I need to make, organized like a UPS route, with the fewest possible left turns. He took the time to circle a couple of fast-food joints along the way. I agreed to Harvey's plan with no intention of following it to the letter. Who did he think he was dealing with? No way I'm eating fast food. It's sit-down dining or nothing at all.

Before I go any further, let's you and me take a trip down TSA Lane.

The thing about the TSA and pot is, they don't want to deal with it. It's outside their mandate, their options are limited.

Be aware I don't endorse any of this behavior. I did it, yes, but here's where I tell you to do as I say, not as I did. And I'm sayin' don't any of this. If you go to jail, too bad, it's on you.

While the TSA screens every bag and every passenger who passes through the security line, checked luggage gets automated screening for things like bombs and weapons and hidden pets. The TSA also does random physical, hands-on, open-up-your-bag-and-rummage-around screening of checked luggage. You'll know this happened to your checked bag because they leave a nice note for you telling you they rifled through your stuff and didn't find anything but your dirty underwear. You are not a terrorist, have a nice day.

What do they do if they find pot, either in your carry-on or your checked bag? They turn you over to the local authorities. Here's where things can get dicey. If you're in a jurisdiction where pot is still illegal, you're screwed. Accept it, be nice to the officers, and get yourself a lawyer. If, on the other hand, you're in a jurisdiction where pot is legal, someplace like, say, Boston, it all comes down to how much you have.

Take note, I have never carried a controlled substance through Boston Logan airport. I'm using it as an example because I fly through there every year on my way to the Summer Decadence in Provincetown known as Carnival. If you've never been, don't go. It's already too crowded and I don't need your competition. For space, for men, for booze, for a dinner reservation, none of it. You should all stay home.

If you're caught with pot of any form in Boston, the TSA will call the Boston PD. As long as you're under the legal limit for possession, they won't arrest you. They don't let you keep it, but you get to go on your merry way. This is the standard practice in the 'pot is legal here' parts of the country, as I understand it. Which is why the police are rarely called for these incidents anymore, in places where pot is legal. If, however, you happen to get snagged with more than the legal limit, and the police are called, you are up a creek, go find a paddle.

Which is what happened to me.

Reminder, Harvey insisted I make it a day trip. People were suffering, I hadn't been in a while, yada blah blah yada. I threw a few basic items into my over-head-bin-sized suitcase, grabbed a bag for my laptop and some other crap I wasn't going to use, and off I went. With ten grand of Harvey's money.

Ten thousand dollars may not be much to you, but it turns out it was a boatload of money to Harvey, and, if I'm being honest, a pretty big chunk of change to me. It didn't occur to me to wonder where he got it. It's how my brain works. Remember, an average trip involved about a thousand dollars. Ten grand, one day, sure, no problem. Off I went.

My favorite seat in first class, seat 1D, is the window seat at the front. People who lean their seat back infuriate me, but I like to do it, so no complaints. Instead, I sit at the bulkhead.

My bag inside my empty suitcase, suitcase in the overhead, then four hours of being treated like a prince.

Not a prince, but three double vodkas, a hot meal, and all the snacks I can eat is close enough. Not exactly the hard knock life. My flight took off at 9:00 a.m. Atlanta time, which put me at my destination well before lunch, local time. I pick up my rental car (whatever the biggest, newest SUV on the lot happened to be when I arrive) and off to work I go.

On a normal trip, if there is such a thing, I have a hotel room and can keep a leisurely pace. The process usually happens over days, not hours. Not this time. I rush around like crazy, loading my vehicle down like a reverse pot Santa, burning through Harvey's cash in about seven hours, give or take a few hours. I then go to my favorite restaurant, before heading to a gas station to fill the tank of my rental.

Doin' great. Next step, pack all the junk I bought. When you buy anything, I don't care what it is, the size of the packaging is always bigger than the actual product. Pot edibles are no different.

I park the SUV at a gas station, hide in plain sight style, and get to work. A mini-van is better for this part of the project, but there's no way in hell I'm driving one of those. Mini-vans are for straight people with kids, not me.

I condense everything down to the fewest number of packages and it doesn't all fit in my suitcase. I ditch all the boxes, but I can't empty all the bottles of THC edibles into one or two big ones because, as Harvey pointed out on multiple occasions, "the handling would be unsanitary."

No worries, I'll put it into my bag, the one I plan to carry on the plane, the one with my laptop I didn't use, the book I didn't read and the snacks I didn't eat. Security has never once looked inside my bag. E-z-P-z.

Done. I head back to the airport, drop off the rental, get to the terminal, check my suitcase at the counter, and step into the security line. My flight leaves in about ninety minutes, plenty of time. I might even get a drink.

When you buy pot edibles, the packaging has all sorts of stuff on the label to indicate, for a whole bunch of good reasons, the contents contain THC. Big pot leaves, big red letters screaming out 'THC,' and other such imagery. There's a complete 'this is pot' iconography. It doesn't show up when they scan your bag. In my case, I forgot to take out my laptop. Lucky me, I get special treatment, aka 'enhanced screening.'

They pull me aside, open the bag, find the edibles, and sequester me in my own private room until the police arrive. At first, I'm worried about missing my flight. I've done my homework, and I know I am below the local legal limit.

Excluding my checked bag.

Time passes. I start to worry. It could have been ten minutes, could have been ten hours. Time is funny. When you're moving, time moves with you. Likewise, when you're still, time crawls. They let me keep all my personal belongings with me, including my snacks, and pretty soon I'm eating my anxiety.

One cool thing about my favorite airline, aside from the awesome points, is the luggage tracker. Once you check your bag, their mobile app updates you about your luggage. 'Your luggage has been checked in,' followed by 'Your luggage is destined for Atlanta flight blah blah,' and ultimately 'Your luggage has been loaded onto flight blah blah and is ready for departure.' Those aren't the exact words, doesn't matter.

I didn't receive any of those while I was waiting. I wasn't being detained, the nice TSA lady made it clear to me, the TSA was NOT detaining me. I was being asked to wait quietly until the police arrived, who would then decide what to do with me.

Since they let me keep my phone, I decided to use it. I thought about calling BeeBee, then decided against it. Too soon, no reason to alarm him. He didn't even know I was on the trip.

I sent Harvey a text instead. One word, 'busted.'

No response. Not even a coy reply like 'wrong number asshole.' Nothing. He's busy being sick, or helping a friend, or taking a nap. It's coming up on 10:00 p.m. in Atlanta, I let it go.

The police arrive. I am not arrested. I answer their questions, leaving out as much as possible. They took my pot edibles, added up the total THC, admonished me, gently, and sent me on my way. One of them was good looking and I couldn't stop staring at him and smiling. He had a massive bulge in his pants. I mean, baseball cup size. It was big enough to be frightening.

At this point in my story Luke burst my bubble by telling me it was exactly as I described it, protective gear. It seems cops get kicked in the crotch a lot. Bummer.

I got on my flight, downed two doubles before the plane was even loaded, finally got the notification my luggage was on board, and fell into a not-too-restful sleep. The first-class crew woke me for dinner, which I declined, but I graciously accepted three more double vodkas. It takes more at altitude, trust the science. I'm out for the rest of the flight. I was drunk when we landed.

It's a long way from landing to exiting the airport in Atlanta. Baggage claim is, of course, the last stop. After deplaning, I start getting nervous. What if they alerted Atlanta about me? What if the APD is waiting to grab me as soon as I pick up my bag? Don't call me queen, but I do have a penchant for drama.

I have two more drinks at the airport. In addition to being drunk, I become paranoid. I decide to skip baggage claim altogether. To hell with my suitcase, it can go around and around the baggage carousel for the next ten years for all I care. I call a ride-share and get my ass back home. Harvey is waiting for me outside my building.

All I can think is, "What the hell? He can't answer a text but he can camp out at my front door?" I refuse to let him in. We can talk on the street or he can take a hike, it's been a long day.

He's pissed. I mean raging. He's too weak to do more than shake his fist at me. But I know rage when I see it. Harvey wants the claim ticket for my luggage. I have never in my life had to present a claim ticket to get my luggage out of the airport. I pick it up and walk out. But you can't do the same with abandoned luggage. You have to present a ticket to pick it up once they pull it from the carousel. Who knew? Not me.

I couldn't remember where I put the ticket.

At this point, Luke interrupts my monologue again. He has one of those narrow, focused questions.

"Charlie, where's the suitcase?"

I tell him the truth.

"Hell if I know."

CHAPTER NINE

About a Bag

The Atlanta airport is the busiest airport in the world. Occasionally some other airport manages to take over the top spot, but those instances are few and far between, and they never last.

Everyone knows how baggage claim works, or should. What a lot of people don't know is what happens to bags when they are unclaimed. There's a lot of unclaimed luggage at the busiest airport in the world. It falls on the airlines to sort out. They have ninety days to get your luggage to you. It's true whether they lost it, or you didn't bother to pick it up on your way out.

In the latter case, which is my case, if they can't reunite you with your wrinkled up clothes and those miniature toiletries you snagged at your hotel, they can sell your bags to a third party. Where it goes for there is up to the third party. This usually means it lands in what some people refer to as a 'second-hand retail environment.' Also known as a thrift store.

I did not know this. I assumed it stayed at the airport for a while, then eventually got tossed out with the trash. Imagine your suitcase and everything in it could end up being for sale in some dusty old shop right next to the booty from a storage locker auction and a stack of scratched up non-stick cookware, all donated by people who had no idea the thrift store was a for-profit business. Yes, I have been one of those people, but it is not the point.

Luke explained all of this to me. I always say, learn something new every day. Luke also explained I could be in some serious trouble, right before he asked me if I had any plans to go get the suitcase.

Here's what I said in response, verbatim, "No, I am not pickin' up my suitcase. I paid thirty bucks for it at Marshall's, it's not worth a ride to the airport." I know it's not what he meant, I was trying to keep the conversation lively. Luke didn't appreciate my humor. Can't win 'em all.

When the airline needs to get your baggage back to you, they do like any other normal business, they call you. Which is great, if they have your phone number.

Yeah, not great. When I changed service providers, because I wanted a new phone for free, I didn't port over my old number. With the exception of BeeBee, Dez, Harvey, and Luke, I don't care if people can reach me. To be honest, I didn't want to hear from Harvey either. Plus, my number got out to the general public, and people who hated my second book started calling me to complain about it.

Free phone, new number, sign me up. I never bothered to update any of my accounts. No one at the airline could reach me and tell me to pick up my suitcase full of contraband. For once, my failure at adulting has paid off.

"This could be a good thing for you," Luke tells me. "If they ship off your bag for sale, it breaks the chain of custody."

Luke wasn't about to let it happen, not even for a handsome young(-ish) guy like me, no matter how good the sex.

"Then again, if it lands on the market," he said, "some kid could get their hands on it."

"I don't want to go back and get the bag, but Harvey…"

"Harvey put you in the hospital over the contents of your suitcase. I'd like to revisit our agreement. Someone is going to be arrested."

Originally, I thought Luke's motive was to get back at Harvey for sending some guy out to kick my ass on Halloween night. I now learned there was more to it.

"The department has been keeping an eye on Harvey for a while. He's made some shady connections lately. Your suitcase is a drop in the bucket. He's into way more. Meth, coke, opioids, you name it, Harvey is in it."

"I offered Harvey a full refund of his ten grand, less expenses," I said, "Sounded fair to me. I'm glad he rejected it, didn't feel great offering it to him in the first place. My freedom, his money, shared risk."

Saying it out loud made me realize how stupid those words sounded.

"Shared risk maybe," Luke said, "but not even close to equal. He has other business partners, and the money he gave you probably wasn't his."

It was starting to sink it. My ass was in a sling, and not the kind some gay men, not me, have in their basements. If you don't get the reference, I can't help you.

"He's supposed to be dying, where does he find the energy for all this?"

"I don't know, but he's been on a losing streak. Ex-wife took him to the cleaners, business dried up, and yeah, he's dying. It's enough to make anyone desperate. When's the last time you talked to him?"

"He called me a few days before Halloween. He said he'd been thinking about our 'situation' and had some ideas to share. He laid out my options. I could get the luggage and hand it over. I said no way. Then he told me to cough up the baggage claim ticket. I told him, truthfully, I didn't know where it was. Then he said I needed to pay him back his twenty grand."

Luke smirked and shook his head. "Repay, with interest. Sounds about right."

Interest. Harvey had become a bank. More like a pawn shop, with rates like his.

"I said no and he gave me his final offer."

When I didn't continue Luke raised an eyebrow, "And…....?"

"It was all about BeeBee. To Harvey, this was all BeeBee's fault, BeeBee introduced us. It made perfect sense to Harvey, but it was batshit crazy to me. How could we be miles apart in our understanding of this situation?"

"At least he's giving you choices," Luke said, without smiling.

Harvey had a pretty good idea about my friendship with BeeBee. One way or another, Harvey would have his pound of flesh. Yes, he used those words, but I doubt he knew it was Shakespeare.

I am no hero. I'm not one to fall on my sword for anything or any person, other than myself, and Brian Barkin. "He said if I didn't come through, he would take it out on BeeBee. He didn't get specific, but his intent was clear enough. I told him to give me a week to figure it out, it was the best counter I could come up with."

"He gave you a week."

"He said 'One week,' then he hung up."

"The assault on Halloween night…"

"Four days after the call. And for the record, I do know how to fight. I grew up gay in the south, fighting came with the territory. But I never saw his first punch coming."

"A lot of other people saw it happen, based on my

interviews."

"It happened fast, I was stunned. I felt like I hung there, like gravity inverted for a few seconds. Once I hit the ground he moved in, and you saw the results. You know, I tore my place apart looking for the claim ticket. No luck. It was Halloween, I had a costume to finish, and I had a few days left to solve this baggage claim problem. I set it aside, I wanted to enjoy my night out. Didn't quite work out the way I planned."

"Didn't he look out of place to you?"

"I wasn't paying attention to him. I was in my Dorothy costume, BeeBee is a fabulous Glinda, we're heading into Xanadu for our Big Gay Halloween Hoedown, and some guy calls out my name. Not Dorothy, Charlie Barnes. In my mind, everybody loves me. Why wouldn't they? Glinda on her stilts didn't notice either, she kept stalking her way through the crowd outside the club."

"Some guy asks me, 'You Charlie Barnes?' and he seems happy to see me, I figured he's a fan. I do have a few. But it sounded like this one's first language was something other than English. Russian, Albania, Greek, I wouldn't know one from the other. I said, 'you bet, what can I do for you?' and his whole demeanor changed."

I try to imitate the accent. "He says, 'Don't want shit. Have message from Harvey. I give taste of what happen when clock run out.' Then bam wham slam, I'm gettin' my ass handed to me."

"He told you Harvey sent him, that he worked for Harvey, interesting."

"Interesting, sure, I'll take your word for it. I will say, right after the first punch a voice in my head said, 'Harvey is not the person you think he is.' At some point, I fell to the ground, he kicked me in the ribs. I rolled away, he planted his heel in my nose. My head hit the pavement, the lights went out."

We've have arrived back where we started. We're all caught up.

Luke and I, still sitting on my sofa, middle of the afternoon, and I've told him my entire story. Whether Harvey meant for me to be hospitalized, or not, is not relevant, according to Luke. I'm convinced it does matter.

"Why?" Luke asks.

"Because I should get an extension on my deal with Harvey equal to the amount of time I spent in the hospital. It's logical to me."

Not to Luke.

He becomes earnest, which is worrisome, "Charlie, you don't have a deal with Harvey. You can't have a deal with him."

The next moment was one of those good news/bad news, 'aha' moments. A sudden onrush of fear and remembrance brought on by the realization you've been blind to the truth of your own situation for a long time and suddenly, you could see it with crystal clarity for the first time.

I don't know how to express this to Luke, instead I ask him, "How screwed am I, and does it help I remembered where I put the ticket?"

He's happy for the first time since we started the discussion.

"If you have it, Charlie, it might get you out of this mess. Where is it?"

I get up, walk over to the table in my foyer where I drop all my stuff every day, and pick up my wallet. It's been there since Halloween, it wouldn't fit in my bra.

I have a nice Tumi bi-fold wallet, a birthday present from Dez. Fancy. I know it was expensive because I looked it up on the interweb. I would never spend a lot of money for something to hold my money, but I like it and I keep next to nothing in it.

It has lots of slots for credit cards, I have two and a debit card. There's a plastic window for your driver's license, a place for cash (which I rarely carry), and these two slots, one on each side. They're such a pain in the ass to get anything out of, I never use them.

Unless I'm carrying something I cannot lose. These are always empty. Correction, not always, one is not empty. It holds my baggage claim ticket.

Like I said, I've never needed a claim ticket before, not ever, when I've travelled. When I've gotten one, it ends up in a side pocket of my duffle bag, where it is forgotten until thrown away some time later, along with all the other crap I collected in my side pockets.

While I was sitting in my private room at the airport, waiting for the friendly local police to come and admonish me for trying to get drugs through the security line, I decided I better hide my baggage claim ticket. I slipped it into my wallet. Tucked it right into one of those tight slots and hoped it would never be found. It was more of an impulse than a deliberate, considered, act.

Which is why I forgot about it immediately after putting it there. The drinks on the plane helped. I pull the ticket out of my wallet, not without effort, and present it to Luke.

He doesn't take it.

"You hang onto it, don't lose it again. I'll be right back."

I think he's leaving. Instead, even though it's not quite beer o'clock, Luke, in his infinite wisdom, decides it's time for a break and a cold one. He comes back with two cans of my favorite beer, Creature Comforts Automatic, ice cold. They say it's 'Radiant, Modern, Pillowy.' By 'they' I mean it's printed on the can. I don't know what those words means, all I know is it's damn good beer. I drink lots of it. 'Nuff said.

"What, no glass?" I hate to drink from the can. I don't

know what's touched the thing since it left the brewery.

"Did you know there was beer in the fridge?"

He's got me there. Doesn't matter, I need a glass. I put my wallet and the claim ticket on the sofa and go fetch a glass.

When I come back, Luke's got his phone out and is taking a picture of the ticket. And my wallet, with my driver's license on full display. "What are you doing?" I ask. The stress in my voice should be obvious to him, given how he never heard it before.

"I have a plan," he says, with more cheer than is reasonable. "Sit down, I'll run it by you." He pats his hand on the sofa, I sit.

"Let's hear it, and please don't tell me it involves me doing anything. I'm not up for doing anything. I mean it, nothing."

He laughs his chuckle of a laugh he makes when he doesn't find me amusing, but wants to humor me. We haven't spent much time together, but what we have has been intense. I'm getting to know him.

"Do you think you can manage a phone call?"

"I can try."

Same chuckle. "It's a start, I'll take it." He takes a long drink from his beer. "You got yourself into this mess. I'm willing to help get you out of it, but you have to put as much skin into this part of the game as you already put into the first part, the part without me."

"We've spent most of our time together in some form of undress. I've got plenty of skin in the game." It's my turn to take a long drink. "Okay, detective, what's your plan?"

"Before I tell you, I think it best I come clean with you on a few topics, and tell you a few things you don't know about your pal Harvey."

This sends me headlong toward a full-on panic attack. He was smart to get me drinking.

"I'm all ears."

"When I was a patrol officer, I arrested Harvey."

When he tells me this, bells in the back of my head start to come to life, telling me I need to pay attention. I'm seeing dots, not before my eyes. I'm seeing dots in my memory, all of which need connecting. Believe what you want, I'm not a reporter and I'm not accountable for any of these details about Harvey. I'm merely a messenger.

This is what Luke told me. I'm giving you the condensed version, we don't have all day.

Harvey was a small-time drug dealer with big-time aspirations. He came from a working-class family, had a chance to go to college on an academic scholarship, and blew it when he got busted for breaking and entering. He and some buddies broke into one of those warehouse-sized arcade places, the ones with go-carts, bowling alleys and bouncy houses, all under one roof. He and three of his best buds from high school got high one night and decided it would be a great idea to bust into one of these places and race go-carts.

Experts who say the human brain is nowhere near fully developed until a person is somewhere in their twenties are right. A bit earlier for girls, often later for boys. There must be an evolutionary theory to explain it. Regardless, for me it makes sense. If we don't need to grow up fast, why would we?

Harvey and his friends' behavior proves the point. They could have gone to the place during normal business hours and spent twenty bucks for their joy rides. But no, to them, breaking and entering, while high, was the better approach.

They break in but can't get the go-carts started. Either too high or too ignorant of the ways of internal combustion engines, it's a toss-up. By the time they give up on their dream of a high-speed adventure, the police are waiting for them outside.

All four of them get caught, but Harvey was the one

holding what was left of their stash. Let's add possession of a controlled substance to the laundry list of crimes.

You might think kids in the suburbs would get off easy, parents are model citizens, cousin is a lawyer, there's no significant infrastructure for juvenile incarceration, take your pick. It's all true. Usually.

Harvey was eighteen. His parents spent everything they had to keep him out of jail. When it was all said and done, he got community service and his parents paid back his measure of the damages, plus a fine. No college for Harvey. He did his community service, then took a job in construction, promising to pay his parents back. He liked the work, and his boss liked him. He kept at it until a recession hit and he was out of job.

Harvey started dealing during this time. He had his own apartment in Atlanta and managed to keep paying his bills, without any visible means of support. One day, he sold some joints to the wrong guy. A young cop working undercover.

A cop named Luke Goode.

"I had a chance to do work any young cop would be excited about. When they offered, I jumped."

"Once we had Harvey, they offered him a deal, to flip on his supplier."

It was no surprise to me, we've all seen the movie. Bust a low-level guy, he turns on the next guy up the chain, and it's onward and upward. Harvey gets busted, makes a deal, spends a couple of weeks behind bars, and gets out of jail with exactly zero prospects.

"Of course he went back to dealing."

Of course.

"I was back on patrol the second time I had an encounter with Harvey, pure coincidence, dumb luck, call it what you want."

It struck me as one hell of a coincidence. I chose to believe him because I'd rather not think about the alternative. Luke pulls him over for a busted taillight, recognizes Harvey, who does not recognize Luke, who searches the car and finds a baggy full of perfectly rolled joints. Down Harvey goes for possession with intent to distribute.

Here comes another one of those dots I mentioned.

"I swear, Charlie, the bag weighed over an ounce when I booked it into evidence. I did not screw up the report."

Interesting. A big-ass dot, don't you think?

The guy who arrested the guy who got out of jail and got a settlement thanks to Brian Barkin, the guy who put the guy who went to jail in jail in the first place, is sitting on my sofa. After having spent the night with me.

Let me rephrase. Luke arrests Harvey. Brian prosecutes Harvey. Brian checks the evidence after the fact. Harvey gets out of jail, and gets a big pay day. Luke becomes a narcotics detective.

It's enough to make my head spin, which, admittedly, is a low bar to clear.

"What do you think happened?" I ask, because Luke is staring straight ahead and not talking. I can hear the gears cranking in his head, but his lips aren't moving. While I wait for my answer, I do consider the alternative, this is an ego-driven vendetta on Luke's part.

"At first I blamed Brian."

Ouch.

"And?" I can't believe how calm I am in this moment. BeeBee is many things, but none of them involve tampering with evidence.

"No. No. Something else happened. I think someone with access to the evidence locker thought they could take a few joints out and no one would ever notice."

"You a think a cop did it?" I'm incredulous, which he picks up on, and seems grateful for.

"No. But it's not important. What's done is done."

Not a vendetta, I'm thinking.

"It chaps my ass."

Luke swears. First I've heard him swear, in anger. We're back to vendetta.

"Luke, I'm confused. I'm not following the timeline here. Harvey got out of jail years ago…"

He sees where I'm going and cuts me off.

"I was already a detective when we met."

"You lied to me."

"No, I didn't," he says.

I wait for the explanation.

"When I told you I made detective, I never said when. You assumed I meant some time since the night we meant."

It's my turn to stare at the wall and think deep thoughts. I'm connecting the dots. "You were in uniform."

"It was easier," he tells me.

"Easier how?"

"A guy in uniform blends in on a night like Halloween. My other options were a costume, or street clothes, neither of which would have served my purpose."

"Which was?" I ask, but I think I know the answer.

"Surveillance."

"You were following me?"

I'm surprised when I realize he's surprised by this.

"Not you. Brian. You were a happy accident."

"Come again?" I'm holding out hope he's about to say something like 'I never would have met you otherwise' or some other sweet romantic nonsense.

"Charlie, you're the key to all of this. You're a mule. With your help, we can take down Harvey's entire operation."

I'm a mule. I'm the key. Harvey has an 'operation.' A whole new page of dots. I wonder what else I am.

"Am I going to jail?"

"Probably not. We'll figure it out."

I am not reassured.

"Are you working?" I ask, because, yeah, it feels like it.

"One thing you have to know about me, Charlie, I'm always working. It comes with the job."

I think I finally know what the word 'gob smacked' means. "Were you working last night, and this morning?" And damn, I think I'm about to cry. It's not like me to shed a tear. All the same, I feel it. Being used is the worst. Something inside me is breaking. Not like glass shattering, more like a Georgia pine bending under the weight of ice and snow. There's this distinct moment, it makes a specific sound, then boom, it's over.

Luke leans towards me, puts his hand on my shoulder, and says in such a gentle, reassuring, and convincing voice, "No Charlie, I told you it was fun time and I meant it. I guess I'm not always working." He smiles when he says this. I see it out of the corner of my eye but I can't look at him, not yet.

"Is there anything else I should know, before we take this any further?"

Luke takes his hand away, leans back, looks down at his own hands, then at the wall, then finally at me. He waits, then speaks quietly, "Charlie, look at me."

Which I do, even though I don't want to.

"I'm not gay."

CHAPTER TEN

Keep it Real

In a way, I'm glad he told me, when he told me. My sadness was obliterated by anger. The last time I felt such a level of anger was in high school, the day my baseball coach called me a faggot at practice.

I loved baseball. Still do. I dreamed of spending my entire life playing baseball. I didn't care if I never made money at it. It's true what they say, enjoy what you do and you'll never work a day in your life. I hit him as hard as I could. Didn't knock him out but knocked him on his ass. South, gay, that's the way it was. We covered this. I never played baseball again. And no one in my school ever called me names again. It was a lousy trade-off, but I accepted it.

I learned a long time ago violence is not the way. It's not the answer. But times like this moment, with Luke on my sofa having dropped a thermonuclear explosion into my lap, it can be hard to hold back.

I manage. But not without raising my voice. I start shouting. I'm standing while I'm shouting. I'm sure I looked like a complete psycho. Who wouldn't?

"What do you mean, not gay? Straight guys don't do the

things you did with me, twice no less. Not when they're sober anyway. Straight guys don't make dinner for gay guys they hardly know. They don't parade around my kitchen half naked. They damn sure don't share my last clean towel. Who are you? What the hell is going on?"

He sits there and listens, letting me burn out like prairie fire.

Which I do, eventually.

When I fall silent and drop back onto the sofa, he asks "Want another beer?" Like we're watching a football game and a commercial came on.

"I think it's a good time for a few martinis."

"Let's stick with beer," he says, and gets up to fetch it. "Want a fresh glass?

Luke acts as though everything is hunky dory and we're all fine and good and let's have another beer and, are you kidding me he's 'not gay?' What have I done?

I tried to think of something snarky to say, but for once words fail me. "Of course I want a fresh glass, I'm not a Neanderthal."

He comes back and hands me a beer and a glass. He can't be bothered to pour? I give him a look to get the message across. He says what I need to hear.

"You're a big boy Charlie, you can handle it."

I assume he's talking about the beer, but there could a double entendre in there.

I pour my beer, take a drink, and have to know, "How could you be straight? I don't get it. The sex… you're good at it. I mean, full-on, get some with gusto, good at gay sex."

He laughs, a genuine laugh, and says, "I'm bisexual."

Bisexual.

"I've always thought bisexuals were a myth, like unicorns and leprechauns."

"There are studies indicating it's the most common form of

sexual expression."

"How clinical. You said your son knows you're gay."

"Your words, not mine. I didn't see the point in getting into it over the phone. What's the difference? My sexuality is not who I am, it's part of the picture, nothing more."

"Are you using me?" I need the truth. I know I've been a stranger to the truth many times in my life, but in the moment, I want truth to be my new best friend.

"No, Charlie," and it sounds like this question hurts his feelings. "I like you. I'm into you. I think there's potential here, for you and me."

"But there'll always be potential for someone else, won't there?" Truth is, he's not the first bisexual person I've ever met, not even the first one I've ever slept with. He is, however, the best, sexually speaking, bisexual I've ever slept with. There's a lot to like about Luke Goode. I'm struggling.

"It's true for every relationship, gay, straight, or bi, always true. When I commit, I commit. There's no in-between or gray area. I don't know if we'll get there or not, but if we make a run at a relationship, it will be you and me. No third parties, no outside friends with benefits. I believe in monogamy."

"Serial monogamy," and I don't care if it stings. It should.

"If you want to label it, fine, we'll label it."

I know what I want. I want to roll the clock back twenty-four hours and start this all over again. I'd do a few things differently, or not at all.

"Where do we go from here?"

"We could go to the bedroom and I could demonstrate my level of commitment again."

"Too soon," I tell him, knowing he was trying to lighten the mood. It's nice he tried.

"You've told me your truth, and I've told you mine. If you want to go forward from here, we need to sort out this Harvey business and see where it lands," he says.

Luke is working again.

"You mean where I land?" This would be hard for Luke and me, if I'm in jail.

"I was kidding earlier. You're not going to jail. Geez, sometimes I wonder what happens to your sense of humor."

This elicits a glare from me, which has the desired effect. We need to keep it real.

"Okay, okay, I'm sorry, you're right, too soon. Feelings, I get it. You're not going to jail. I've got a plan. To be fair, you made this bed, you'll have to help."

"What's next?" I'm defeated. Or tired from the beer.

"You've had the history lesson, it's time for current affairs."

I'm hungry. I feel like I've spent my entire life sitting on my sofa, talking with Luke. It's been a few hours, but damn, what hours they've been. Before he can dive into the next round of revelations I ask, "Are you staying for dinner?"

"Do you want me to?"

"Are you cooking?"

"I can."

"Then let me change the question. What are we having for dinner?"

Why do I care? Because I'm starting to think he cares. And because I'd rather move forward than stay stuck in a place where I'm angry and sad and worried.

A smile sweeps across his face, "I'll figure something out."

Great, he's happy. I hope I catch up. "Current affairs?"

"Yeah, I think we need to get everything on the table, before we talk about dinner." He's right, again. Why does he get to be right all the time? Must be genetic. He was born with all the 'I make good decisions' genes. I think I've seen, and connected, enough dots to know what Luke is going to tell me. I decide it's best to let him tell me.

"Harvey's the one who's been using you."

"No, you think? What gave you such an idea?"

"Don't be snippy. It's not like you figured it out yourself."

He's got me there. Right again. Damn.

"How used have I been?"

The story, as told by Detective Luke Goode, takes two hours. I don't want to write it all out. Let's go with the condensed version.

There are no sick people. There were at first, that's really where we started. But now, there are no charity cases out there, waiting for help with their chemo side-effects. Harvey is the exception, not the rule. Harvey has been reselling, at substantial markup, most of the goods from my shopping trips, since long before I formed our LLC. He made a genuine business of it. The market for high quality edibles is strong in metro Atlanta, which is why he upped the ante. Harvey's process is straightforward. Take the bottles, separate them into smaller amounts, sell them at a huge markup. By Luke's estimate, my suitcase is worth at least fifty thousand dollars to Harvey.

Am I a dumb ass? Why yes, I am. Gullible, naive, self-indulgent. All of the above, guilty as charged. Luke tries to make me feel better, but it's an uphill battle.

Based on Luke's investigation, Harvey made some commitments he can't meet, not without the suitcase. Harvey's willing to hurt BeeBee to get me to do his bidding. I honestly feel grateful he sent his goon at me first. Harvey has no idea who he's up against. I'm not talking about Luke. I'm talking about me. I'm not perfect, but I'm loyal. I'll do anything to protect BeeBee. If it means sending Harvey to prison, I'll do it. If I go down with him, I'll have to come to terms with it.

I have Luke on my side. Also, the entire narcotics division of the Atlanta PD, a contingent of the Georgia Bureau of Investigation, and the United States Drug Enforcement

Administration, are also in my corner. The GBI is involved because of their local labs and a multi-jurisdictional oversight, and the DEA jumped in because it's an interstate affair. It's all a bit much to accept, even with Luke's reassurance.

In addition to the size of the trade Harvey's been doing, it's the customers. Kids. One of Harvey's minions sold drugs to a high school kid, who sold it to another kid, who got caught with it and turned his buddy in. The police did their thing, worked their way up the ladder until they got close to Harvey. Of course, our pot edibles racket was the tip of the iceberg. One product in a much larger product portfolio. A low risk, steady revenue product. And the Russian-not-Russian guy who paid me a visit? Complete fraud. I got smacked down by a fake Russian.

I've never been a 'professional' wrestling fan, which is why I didn't recognize him. Gerry Bergdoff. Former small-time pro wrestler who couldn't make it in a fake sport, he became a fake strongman for Harvey. Yeah, I said it. Fake sport. Fake as hell. Pro wrestling is fake. You can enjoy it if you want, but don't tell me it's a real sport. Stop reading and walk away if you disagree.

I guess Harvey decided if he was gonna die, he was goin' out with a bang. Coke, ecstasy, opioids, mushrooms, pot, and of course, his most recent product, pot edibles. He drew the line at crack. I don't know why, how could I? I didn't know any of this.

"I assume Harvey had bills to pay, and no way to pay them, but would it be enough to drive a guy to this level of criminality?"

"He's got a kid. Not with his wife, long before they divorced. The theory is, he wants to leave something for her, wants her to have some financial security. Or it's as simple as old habits die hard."

"The shit around Harvey keeps getting deeper. I'm stuck right there with him, up to my knees in it." Shame. I know it well. I've never been this ashamed.

Well, yes, I've been this ashamed before. It's a story for another time.

"There's hope for you yet, a chance for redemption."

I believe him. I've decided to trust him. Truth has a way of making trust happen, especially the painful truth.

Luke has a plan. He's got it all figured out. He has to sell it. To his boss, to the GBI, and most importantly the DEA. He believes he can get it done. He sold me on more than one notion already, didn't he? Literally had me eating out of his hand.

Dinner. By the time Luke tells me Harvey's truth, I'm starving, and hopeful. Hopeful Luke will cook me dinner, he'll spend the night again, and he'll make all of this go away, and soon. If I have to settle for two out of three, I hope it's the right two. He laid out his plan. He made dinner. And he spent the night.

It's gonna sound cheesy, but it was nice to have him spend the night without any expectations. Two out of three. He was gone when I woke up.

Luke's plan is straightforward, when you get down to it. The tricky part involves me not spending the next decade in prison. He left me a note, right to the point, as is his way:

Charlie,

Gone to work. Will call around 1.

Breakfast in the fridge.

Luke

The 'PS' was the good part. It made my morning.

PS, last night was nice. L.

I found a bagel and some cream cheese in the fridge, made some coffee, and proceeded to burn the bagel. An 'everything' bagel smells awful when it burns, did you know this? It's a good early warning sign, when the kitchen starts to stink.

Luke's plan. Simple. I will give Harvey the claim ticket. This has to be observed, preferably recorded. Still some logistics to work out on this part. Then Harvey has to go get the bag. Or one of his peeps has to get it, then deliver it to Harvey. Then Harvey has to sell some of the bag's contents to an undercover who's never purchased from Harvey before. A problem, but, I assume, not mine to solve.

Prerequisites, there are a few. Luke needs receipts for the contents of the suitcase. What he needs is an inventory of what's in the bag. Which would be easy if the receipts weren't in the suitcase. OK, modify the plan. Luke says he can handle it. Get a warrant, get someone to go to the airport, they open the bag and take pictures of the receipts and the goods. Sounds easy, primarily because, again, I don't have to do it. There are lots of details, but my part is practically miniscule. Assuming I get immunity.

It's Tuesday morning and I have not left my place since getting home from the hospital. I'm feeling pretty good and the weather is nice, I decide to have my breakfast on my covered balcony, because I have a balcony, why not eat there? It's is a good day for a walk in the park. My face is more yellow than purple and, at this point, I don't give a damn who sees me anymore.

I'm sipping my coffee after eating my super-crunchy bagel smothered in schmear, when I start to feel something isn't right. Although our building has a small parking lot behind it, most of my neighbors park on the street during the day, usually when they come home for lunch. It's such a pain in the ass to navigate the tight spaces in the lot. This is how I know everyone's car.

I also know, generally speaking, when they go to work and

come home from work. I don't have to schlep into an office every day because my office is next to my living room.

Tuesday morning, the street should be empty. And it's not. Neither is the car. There's a guy in the driver's seat. Am I paranoid or is he looking at my front door? He's parked down the street, facing away from the front of my building. I can see a face in the side mirror, looking back toward me. Time for a closer look. But I'm not walking down there though, I'd have to get dressed.

I have binoculars. Think what you want, I had them long before I moved into my place. I like birds. Once upon a time, I was an outdoorsy type, I bought some nice Bushnell binoculars, and what's it to you if it's not birds I look these days? I keep them on a bookshelf on my balcony. Not much good if I have to go track them down.

Back to the car. I look. I look again. And to be certain, I take another long look. It's the fake-sport fake Russian, Gerry Bergdoff. I'm surprised. Harvey is a cheap bastard, this guy has to be costing him…something. I wonder how long he's been out there, sitting in his beat-to-shit Volvo station wagon, staring at my front door? I'll show you, turd blossom. I take a picture of the car and text it to Luke with the message 'I've got company. Gerry's outside.'

I don't know why I expected an instant response. It took at least five minutes for Luke to get back to me.

'Stay inside.'

I feel compelled to go for a walk. I won't be trapped in my home by this guy. Then another text from Luke, this time, I'm intrigued.

'Wait twenty minutes, then walk. Crescent to 10th, head to park. Stop at FO. Meet you there. Make sure he sees you.'

OK, there's all kinds of stuff wrong with this. First, those directions take twice as long. Second, I have to walk even further down 10th, one of the busiest cross streets in the city. I hate it, at least until it gets to the park, where it's nice and I don't hate it. Third, FO is for the Flying Omelet. The Flying Omelet, are you kidding? He can't do better? I think he can.

No offense to the Flying Omelet, but the chain doesn't hold a candle to the original in Candler Park. History lesson for today: The original Flying Omelet opened in Candler Park, once a hotbed of Lesbians with Money. It may still be, I don't know, haven't been there in a while. If it's like everything else we gays build up, it's probably all been taken over by upwardly mobile couples and their perfectly dressed, upwardly mobile babies.

The Flying Omelet was this amazing breakfast joint with a Blue Girl as one of the founders. Blue Girls, famous for folksy-rock numbers. I was at a fancy art opening one night, getting along famously with a young female musician who describe herself as a folk artist.

I mentioned the Blue Girls and she had no idea who they were. I was outraged. I decided to sleep with her boyfriend, to teach her a lesson. Last I heard, she brought down the house with a rendition of 'Ghost.' Seems I did her a favor.

The Original Flying Omelet, Candler Park. Their bakery next door was second to none. I mean, if you couldn't get a table for breakfast, you'd happily wait in line for anything, literally anything, from the bakery.

There was this pastry chef there named Georgie who made the place special. Whenever I walked in and Georgie was there, I knew I'd get a smile, and the conversation would go something like, "How ya' doin', thanks for comin' in, here's yah blueberry scone, have a nice day, y'all come back." For those not from the south, we say "y'all" whether there's one of y'all or ten of y'all.

Georgie was awesome. I hated what happened to him on reality TV.

The place sold and became a chain. It's never been the

same and I have no idea what became of Georgie, not after he was on the cooking show with the raging chef. I'm not saying the chain store version of the Flying Omelet isn't good, it's good. The cheese grits with a buttermilk biscuit smothered in pig-based gravy together make up the World's Greatest Hangover Cure. But no matter how many locations they open, you can never get a table when you want one. And they ain't cheap, not like the Golden Skillet. If Luke wants to meet there, fine, I'll meet him there. I'll leave five minutes later and make him sort out the seating.

The fourth thing wrong with Luke's instructions. 'Make sure he sees you.' I guess it takes leaving through the back door off the table. My condo doesn't have a back door, in the strictest sense. I have a door from my laundry room onto a steel balcony connecting to the fire escape/staircase.

This would take me down to a semi-private courtyard with a breezeway leading to the parking lot. It would be easy to leave without being seen, assuming no one's watching the backside of the building. It would also be the fastest way to get to the park.

Not today. Today I follow instructions from Luke, which is definitely becoming a habit, and get myself ready to take my walk. By 'get myself ready' I mean put on clothes. I'm still in my robe, as I should be before noon.

I step through the door of my building and stand outside on the landing, looking up at the sky, thinking this is the best way to make sure Gerry the Freak sees me. Crescent is directly across from me. I set off at a brisk pace, trying not to look like I know I'm supposed to be followed.

I get a text message. Luke.

'Slow down.'

What? He's supposed to be ordering me a coffee and a biscuit. I hate walking slow. In New York, if you walk slow you die. It sucks because, if you're a tourist, you want to take it all in.

In Atlanta, if you walk slow, you don't die. People walk around you. Some of them even say 'excuse me.' Still, there's no reason to walk slow. There's not much to take in and the point of walking is it's a pain in the ass to drive if you're going to the park. There's no place to park, at the park.

Another thing you can get away with in Atlanta, crossing mid-block. There are these pedestrian 'safe havens' all over the place to allow walkers to stop traffic whenever they're too lazy to walk to the end of the block and use a proper crosswalk.

Crescent is a short, angled avenue from my street to 10th street. It pops out next to the MARTA station. MARTA is Atlanta's subway. It's awesome as long as you're not going anywhere. I'm being unfair. I don't know, I never use it, it's what I hear from other people who don't use it.

The conversation usually goes something like this, 'Oh, you live near the MARTA station on tenth, must be convenient.'

'Why?'

'You can hop right on the train.'

'Do you ever take MARTA?'

'No, but I hear it's nice.'

'Why not, if it's nice?'

'I guess it doesn't go where I need to go. Besides, I like to drive.'

And people wonder why the system is always short of money and traffic in Atlanta sucks.

I get to 10th and look to my left to see the lights in the mid-block crosswalk are red and flashing, someone has stopped traffic. As I do this, I notice the beat-up Volvo sitting a few cars back.

Perfect. I make my own crosswalk and trot across to the north side of tenth, then turn right to head toward the park, by way of the Flying Omelet. I saved myself at least one red light, which makes me a genius. I catch the 'walk' sign on Peachtree Street, which changes when I'm halfway across. Gerry the Fraud gets stuck at the light. I slow my pace.

Peachtree Street. World Famous Peachtree Street. People say, and they're right to say it, damn near every street in and around Atlanta has the word Peachtree in it. There's West Peachtree Street, North Peachtree Street, Old South Peachtree Street, and my favorite, New Old South Peachtree Street. My list barely scratches the surface.

The best part about Peachtree is it's all a big marketing con. It used to be 'Pitch Tree Street.' Pitch, as in pine tar, ergo pitch tree is another name for pine tree. Pitch had all kinds of industrial uses back in the day, still does, in fact. Tar paper, charcoal briquettes, all sorts of cute stuff. It was a major product back when the city entered its first boom, but didn't fit with the image the high-and-mighties - socialites, politicians and business people - of the future Atlanta envisioned for a growing city.

A long time ago Atlanta wasn't called Atlanta. It had a couple of names before Atlanta, Marthasville among them. Some railroad engineer - Atlanta was, and still is, a rail hub - offered up 'Atlantica-Pacifica' as the new name for Marthasville.

Someone less technical, less railroad-focused, shortened it, and Atlanta was born. Probably the same person who decided 'Peachtree' was more pleasant and marketable than 'Pitch Tree,' and they were right again.

I think through all these iterations on Peachtree, and all this history, as I'm walking. It helps me avoid looking around for Luke. He's gotta be here someplace. I don't think I'm supposed to see him. I even manage to not check for Gerry the Faker of All Things.

Yes, I am bitter. No apologies.

I get to Piedmont Avenue, the restaurant is across the street, and I get another text from Luke, 'In back next to b-r.' There is something wrong with Luke if he thinks it's okay to sit next to the bathroom in a restaurant. This breaks the number one rule I have about eating out. Don't sit near the bathroom. If I come to your eatery and the available tables are by the toilet, tell me, and I'll walk out without taking a pointless tour of your dining room. 'Better table?' I text back.

It's not about hygiene, though hygiene matters. It's about the traffic pattern. The Flying Omelet is small and everyone who takes a leak will have the opportunity to bump into me. Both ways, coming and going. It's no way to enjoy a meal. I consider skipping this rendezvous completely when I get his reply. 'Out of view.'

OK, I can make a sacrifice. I can compromise my standards for safety's sake, when it's my safety. And Luke's, I guess. He doesn't want Sir Fakes-A-Lot to see us. Got it. The light changes and I cross the street and step into the restaurant's vestibule. I hear, then see, the Volvo speed up as it heads down the street and makes a quick swoop into a parking space along the curb.

I step inside. Mission accomplished.

CHAPTER ELEVEN

Table for Two, for Now

"Hello handsome."

I smile inside every time Luke says this to me. I barely know him, could be he says it all the time to every guy he meets. I will pretend he says it to no one but me.

He's tucked in at a table for two, precisely adjacent to the door to the men's room. He was wise enough, or lucky, to take the closer of the two chairs and leave me the one with some breathing room. I sit. He mistakes my relief at this seating arrangement as something related to Fat Faker in his Crappy Swedish Station Wagon.

Alright, alright, I'll stop with the names. It feels good, which means it's wrong and bad karma.

"Stressful walk?" he asks, raising his eyebrows, demonstrating what might be genuine interest. This is a good move on his part. It makes his manly face look boyish, which might sound weird, but it's not. Believe me on this one. All men are still boys at heart, and it's nice to see it in a face now and again. Especially one with perfect dark eyebrows, a short haircut, and shockingly blue eyes.

"No," I reply, telling part of the truth. "He's parked down

the street, on the right, about five or six cars down from Drake's."

Drake's, for those interested, has been a straight-friendly house of ill repute since 1988. It's an institution unto itself, and one of my favorite places to get a drink, as long as it's not too late. They have everything; drag, karaoke, DJs, you name it. I don't know how they do it, the place has less square footage than my condo. It's why it always feels packed.

I'm thinking I'll drop in and visit Tommy at the bar after my walk. He's the best, and works the first shift. His reasoning is solid. Why work your butt off at night when you can put out a tenth of the effort for fifty percent of the tips? I like Tommy, he's smart.

"Charlie, I need you to focus. I need you to be present."

He's reading lips again. I might have to hate him for his parlor trick. We'll see. "OK, I'm here. What's next?" I ask, because I have no clue what's going on.

"We eat."

"I had breakfast, you left it for me. Do you want me to get fat?" I mean it, all I have to do is think about biscuits and gravy and my ass starts expanding. It's big enough already, thank you. Baseball, I mentioned this before. I played catcher. Constant up and down, it builds a guy's backside like no other sport, except hockey, without all the weight lifting. Squats are no fun when there's an iron bar on your shoulders; repetitive motion gets the job done equally as well.

Luke laughs his 'I'm pretending to be amused' laugh and says, "I can't imagine you ever being fat Charlie. You've got good genes."

Ugh. If he meant it, it would be an okay compliment. Since I know it's bullshit, it's lame. Something's wrong. I mean, I know a lot is wrong, but there's something new wrong. Let's get to it. Before I can speak, he cuts me off and says, "I ordered for you."

What did you order? Complete the thought, Luke. This is weird.

"What's going on?" I don't care what he ordered. The waitress arrives, refills his coffee and fills a cup for me.

"Hi Charlie, nice to see you, it's been forever."

I try to be cheerful. "Hi Bella, I've been away for a bit."

"Mr. Delicious here already ordered for you. Such a sweet man. Back in a flash with your food. Nice to see you again."

Luke is looking at his phone. I'm not sure he even noticed Bella.

"What gives? I'm getting weird-as-hell vibes off you," which is my way of saying put down the phone and talk to me, or I'm going to Drake's for a mimosa.

"Sorry," he says, and tucks the phone into his jacket. "We've got eyes on Gerry, needed to check in."

Silence. Again. Luke is looking at some spot on the wall, a chip in the paint, a leftover glob of dried-up grits. Hard to say. I don't know why I'm getting pissed off. But I am. I force myself to be patient.

Finally, he turns and looks me in my eyes, which has the effect of making me scared and aroused, all at once. This is something I may never get used to. Then he says "It's Brian. I think we've got a problem with Brian."

I sit back in my chair with such sudden force it nearly breaks it. The cracking sound is loud enough to momentarily silence the conversations around us.

"I told you, BeeBee is not involved with any of this."

"I know what you said," he replies, and for a moment I think he's joking. No, he's serious.

"Charlie, I know this is hard for you to hear, but I think, we think, Brian Barkin is more involved with Harvey than he's led you to believe."

No details? I'm not accepting anything until I hear details or see proof.

"In what way?"

"We think Harvey works for Brian."

"Bullshit, no way, I'm not buyin' it," I reply, trying to keep calm, which is not coming easily to me.

"It's possible Brian works for Harvey, but not likely," Luke responds.

"Which is it, Luke, what are you talking about?"

At which point Bella returns with our food, "Egg white omelets and fruit cups all around, you boys enjoy."

Hell no. I take the hideous cup of purple, orange, and yellow and park it in front of Luke. "Bella, cheese grits, home fries, and a titch more coffee for me, please doll."

"You got it Charlie, be right back."

I like fruit, but I don't like fruit at a breakfast joint late morning. In fairness to the Flying Omelet, I've never eaten fruit with breakfast at any restaurant. And of course, I've never gotten sick from the good old FO, are you kidding? Would I be here if I had? Fruit someone else has handled, potentially not washed, with unwashed hands, then dumped in a bowl, and left out in the open, I don't see it as safe. Luke can take the risk, not me.

"You need to reconsider your diet, Charlie. You're not getting any younger," he tells me, as if I didn't know.

I decide not to tell him why I won't eat the fruit. He can figure it out tomorrow, or later today, time will tell.

"How prescient. Talk to me about BeeBee."

"I don't know how much I can tell you. There's been some unusual communication between Brian and Harvey. And there's a financial arrangement we're trying to sort out. I can tell you this, it's not adding up to anything good."

To me, this sounds like a wiretap. Is it even called a wiretap anymore? They're listening to Harvey's phone calls. Money, they're digging into bank accounts, taxes, who knows? Best to play ignorant, which is easy because I am.

"I don't understand."

It's taken me all of two seconds to inhale my omelet, which is not an omelet because it's nothing but egg whites. Bella returns with my real food. Proper Southern grits and home-fries. I love me some home-fries. Hash-browns are better, but hey, we're not at Waffle House, gotta make do.

"Here ya go hon, grits and taters, like you like 'em. And between you and me, I told boy wonder here you wouldn't eat the fruit. He didn't believe me, imagine."

"Imagine," I reply as she moves on to her next table. I dive into my starch and salt with gusto. It takes about a minute.

"I can't give you details, Charlie, not yet. But it doesn't look good. The text I was reading before, it was about Brian. And Gerry, and Harvey. We know Harvey and Brian have a relationship. The connection to Gerry Bergdoff, it's not clear yet."

I drop my voice to a near whisper and lean in, "You can't think Brian is connected to Gerry. No way."

"I haven't seen any evidence he is. Do you know any reason why Brian would give Harvey a large sum of money?"

"No, of course not." I can't even process the concept.

We catch a moment of silence as Bella refills our coffee mugs. The coffee isn't great, in fact it sucks compared to the stuff BeeBee has me drinking, but it's getting the job done. Coffee snob, remember?

"Luke, I have to ask. Are you sure you're not trying to get back at BeeBee for getting Harvey out of jail? Is this a payback situation?" I hit a button. His face turns red, veins start to bulge, eyes narrow. I think he might shoot me. Then, quick as he appeared, the Hulk version of Luke fades away.

"My captain asked me the same question."

"What'd you tell him?"

"I told him I was doing my job, like always. The difference here is I know the players in the game, and I happen to like two of them. One in particular."

I assume he means me, but I want to hear him say it because one, I'm vain, and two, I want to be sure. "You mean me."

"Who else would I mean?"

"Checking. What else can you tell me? Because I gotta say, this does not make any sense to me. BeeBee is a saint. He'd give his right arm if he had to, to do the right thing."

Luke's response is slow, measured, cautious, "It could be a matter of perspective. It could be the right thing is more about what's right for him and for Harvey, even if it's not the right thing to do, strictly speaking. "

It's a lot to think about. How many times have I done what I thought was right for me, too bad if it wasn't right for anyone else, or even legal? While I'm thinking about it, an altogether different thought starts to form. A question, more than a thought. The question is, 'Since I created this mess, shouldn't I be the one to sort it out?'

Put another way, I think I'm tired of screwing around and trusting other people to take care of my mess for me. Time to dig.

"How do you know BeeBee gave Harvey money?"

Luke starts squirming. Not a lot, but enough for me to notice, which is a lot since I haven't seen him squirm before. He wanted my full attention, he's got it. I feel parts of my brain lighting up I didn't know still worked. Interesting. I should drink this coffee more often.

Without looking at me, Luke says "Can you take it on faith I know this?"

"No, this is BeeBee you're talking about. If I'm going take risks for you, to get to Harvey, I need to know why you think BeeBee is involved, and how you know about it. I think it's fair." This is the first time in our short relationship I've pushed Luke. Let's see how this goes. Good times at the

Flying Omelet.

"I can share this," he starts, again slow and cautious, "Brian took a substantial amount of cash out of one of his accounts and gave it to Harvey. We tracked the money all the way to the hand-off to Harvey. It was easy."

"Do tell," I push some more.

"I can't," he says, and looks at me. "And you can't ask Brian. You could tip them both off and we'd be left with only you, and your suitcase."

"I see."

And I do see, for the first time. Like a bolt of lightning before the thunder, everything becomes clarity followed by moments charged silence. It's why the symbol of a good idea, or moment of clarity, is a lightbulb. Everything is suddenly illuminated.

Something is off here. Luke is trying to sell me a mountain of bullshit. If my suitcase is all they have, what happened to all the drug dealing Harvey is supposed to be up to? I think Luke tripped. I'm not sure if I should be hurt or angry, so I allow for both. One thing I should make abundantly clear, I can put up with a lot from a guy, especially if he's handsome, has a great body, and is good in the sack. But I will not put up with attacks on my friends. I have two, BeeBee and Dez. I know I'm not saying much, but I mean it.

A few hours ago, I was planning our wedding. Now, I'm making altogether different plans. Like, how to get out of this place as soon as possible and get in touch with BeeBee before this gets any more out of hand.

"What about Gerry the Ham Fist?" I ask, to keep the conversation moving.

"Let him follow you, we'll follow him, make sure he doesn't come at you" is his answer.

I will play stupid because it's easy and I like easy. "Makes sense," I say, and for added effect, I reach across the table and take his hand and continue, without any hint of sarcasm, which is difficult, "Thank you Luke, it means a lot, knowing you're looking out for me. I hope it's not too much trouble."

He responds exactly as I thought he would and hoped he wouldn't, with his fake chuckle, which I now realize is his way of being condescending. His way of hiding the truth. I know his tell.

"It's what I do Charlie, don't sweat it."

This world I was building in my head is crashing into a heap of rubble and ash, and I want to stand up and run. But I don't. I've been played. I suspected it last night, now I know it. And it's Luke who's playing me. Harvey too, but I'll deal with him later.

It's time to start playing my own game. "What's next?"

"Head back to your place, sit tight. I'll let you know when we have the pieces in place. You should be able to call Harvey tonight, we'll have surveillance in place at the airport by morning. I'll let you know where to arrange the meet with Harvey, and we'll take it from there."

Why thank you Detective Goode, the timeline is helpful. "This is a lot, Luke. It's giving me a headache. Or it's the coffee. I don't know. I need to get some air, and some aspirin. You mind taking care of this? I'm gonna take a walk."

I stand up and he's caught off guard. All I want to do is get out.

"Charlie, I don't…"

"Call me later, I'll be home, waiting to hear from you. Thanks Luke, you're the best," I say as I turn away and head to the door. On the way out I pass close enough to Bella to say "Bella, doll, keep him in his seat for as long you can. I'll make it up to you later."

"Well honey pot, I can't wait to see how you'll manage that," she says, scanning me head to toe. "Don't you worry about a thing, Auntie Bella's on the job."

I'm out the door a second later. A left turn takes me to the park, passing Gerry and his rolling junkyard of a car. Not goin' his direction. I know these streets better than a twenty-dollar rent boy. I turn right, cross back over Piedmont, then head up toward an alley leading back to Peachtree. Halfway up the alley I dive into a parking garage and take the stairs up to the shops and restaurants at street level with Peachtree.

Cut through the lobby, out the other side and down a set of stairs to another parking deck. Pop out the other side of this one, and I'm looking at what was once one of my favorite gay bars in Atlanta, but is now a drug store. A national chain I refuse to name. Exactly what the doctor ordered. I go in, grab a pre-paid cell phone, and I'm back on the street. Head to the back of the parking lot, cut across a vacant lot with a sign announcing the site as the future home of a boutique hotel, and I'm back on Juniper.

The Dakota is across the street. The Dakota is a set of high-end luxury townhomes and condos, developed in the late 80's and intended to appeal to people who were either rich gays, or who didn't mind being surrounded by rich gays. It started a trend. Bars became drug stores, abandoned buildings became lofts, and the twenty dollar rent boys gave way to baby carriages.

It sucks, I know, but it happens. We still out-vote the breeders around here, but our days are numbered.

The Dakota has an inner courtyard. Nice and private. This time of day, few people will be home. This is my destination. I activate my Amazing Wonder Phone from the drug store and call, you guessed it, BeeBee. He doesn't answer. Probably because he doesn't recognize the number. If I know BeeBee, and I do, he'll think this is a scam call and block the number.

Gotta move fast. BeeBee and I, right before we graduated from college, came up with a code word. Back then, you had to pay for text messaging, can you believe it? What a scam.

Code word. We made a pact. If either of us ever needed the other, no questions asked, we would text a code word. The deal was, the recipient had to drop everything, and move heaven and earth to reach the sender. One word, and it had to be something we'd never text to one another for any other reason. A word neither of us liked to use. Something special.

BeeBee invoked this with me when his mother died, which was probably awkward, but he did it. It was the one time we ever needed this.

I type, 'Vagina,' hit send, and wait.

***

I don't have to wait long. Ten seconds, tops.

"How bad?" his first words when I answer.

"Second-to-worst," I reply.

Worst is 'death.' I can't legitimately say worst, not yet. Second-to-worst is 'grave danger, possible grievous harm.' We're there, for sure.

"Location," he demands.

"John Lennon," I reply, and know he'll make the connection.

I'm not being disrespectful of John Lennon. He was murdered in front of The Dakota in New York, where he and Yoko Ono lived. A horrible loss, it should never have happened. And it's the best way to communicate my location. I'm being paranoid, but even paranoids have enemies, some of whom can listen in on phone calls.

BeeBee is a huge fan of John Lennon, he should get this. A few seconds pass before BeeBee responds "On the way. Southeast corner, coming from the east. Five minutes."

Click, call's over.

Five minutes is enough time for me to wonder 'how the hell is he gonna to get here in five minutes?' I wait three minutes, then head to the corner.

A short breezeway connects the courtyard to the corner, not unlike the breezeway in my building, but bigger, nicer, and a lot cleaner. I make note of the fact the developers did a decent job of capturing the old-school vibe they were going for when they built The Dakota (to resemble the ambience of the one in New York, which is old-school by virtue of being old). I could move here one day. Something tells me the laundry rooms aren't an afterthought.

Honk, honk, BeeBee's approaching. Or rather, Dez and BeeBee. She's driving. Is everyone I know driving around midtown for no good reason? Great. This should be interesting. I give Dez two minutes to start harping on me about my non-existent book. They cross the street and stop long enough for me to jump in the back seat. She takes off before I can get my seatbelt fastened.

I don't much care about seatbelt laws, but Dez is a terrible driver. You risk life and limb when you ride with her. She was taking me to lunch one day and drove directly over a big chunk of concrete, like it wasn't even there. She saw it, she even pointed it out before she hit it. After her Suburban stopped shuddering, she said, "Hitting it is safer than swerving." It was a five lane, one way street. With no other cars around.

They both try to speak at the same time. Dez, "Where are we going?" Always practical.

BeeBee, "What's happening, what's the emergency?" Always concerned.

"Turn left," I say without looking up from the damn seatbelt, which is refusing to buckle.

"I can't go left, it's a one way," she shouts.

Why is she frustrated? I'm the one who can't get her car to work.

"Then go straight until you can turn left." Snap. I'm in. I take a deep breath and let it out. "I need to get to the airport, immediately." I try to say this emphatically and it comes out melodramatic, as usual. I deserve the response I got.

"Honey, you're not properly dressed for the airport," she says, "you can't fly in those clothes, the flight crew will think you're a bum. And where are your bags? And what's the emergency?"

"Dez," BeeBee interrupts, "please. Let me handle this."

"Oh well, don't mind me, I'm the driver, nothing more. I might as well put one of those U's in the window and start picking up strangers."

BeeBee has turned around in his seat to face me, which is easy because the Suburban is a land yacht, there's plenty of room to move. I make another mental note, this might come in handy if I ever go car shopping and need a combination grocery-getter and home theater.

"Talk to me Charlie," BeeBee says, with a voice he usually saves for people much more important than me, like Dez. He's all business. This tells me he's worried. He should be.

"It's Luke. He's up to something. I think he's using me to try to set you and Harvey up."

"Are you fleeing the country?" Dez asks, in all seriousness.

"No, of course not," though I know I should consider it.

"I told you there was something fishy about Mister Blue-Eyes," she says, directing this to BeeBee.

He gives her a long look but says nothing, then turns back to me.

"What do you mean?" BeeBee asks, in the same business voice.

"I think he's trying to frame you for drug trafficking, to blackmail you."

This is the moment when I knew my insistence on buckling up was the right instinct.

Dez accelerates. We're approaching a yellow light, and, to Dez, yellow means 'go faster.' She whips the car to the left, tossing BeeBee against the window, oversteering at high speed, sending us into what you might call a drift, if you're being generous. Another over-steer, some more tire screeching sounds, then she gets it under control.

"What's at the airport, Charlie?" she asks, and now she's all business.

BeeBee is recovering from being tossed around the front seat and I blurt out, "Evidence. I have to get there before Luke."

Dez stomps on the gas pedal, demonstrating an amazing hidden feature of the Suburban known as "the kick-down." Other vehicles have this feature, but most of them don't have V-8 engines.

A kick-down is a way of telling your automatic transmission to collaborate with your big-ass engine and go a lot faster, in a hurry. You stomp the gas pedal through the resistance you normally feel in the pedal when accelerating, and off you go. Kick-down, plus ginormous V-8 engine, equals awesome. Unless Dez is driving, in which case it's terrifying.

BeeBee decides he needs his seatbelt and asks, "What are you doing? Are you insane? Slow down Dez."

She screams, "Hell no, nobody's going down on my watch, boys, hang on." She whips the car across an intersection and takes us into downtown proper.

Welcome to downtown Atlanta, where's it's always crowded, even on the weekends.

She takes us up an angled approach to one of the Peachtree streets, then veers to the left, toward some of the Portman towers. Portman, famous architect who designed ugly buildings in Atlanta and San Francisco, some other places. Hate me if you want, but I hate his buildings, we're even.

"Where are you going?" BeeBee shouts back at her.

"HOV onramp near Freedom Parkway, totally legit, there's

three of us." She hooks another left, nearly takes out a pedestrian, and ahead in the distance, like the mountain pass to Shangri-La, is the on-ramp to the southbound HOV lane.

One light to beat and the moment it turns yellow, she hits the kick-down again. We're heading downhill on a narrow street fast enough for people to hear us coming and get the hell out of our way. No mid-block crossings here. We hit the cross street, which sends us airborne for more than a few seconds.

This is a rather interesting sensation. Weightless for a few seconds and right about the time you realize you're gonna feel it when you come down, you do. Boom! We hit the road and something flies off the car and there's a loud metal-on-pavement clanging sound. We survive, and she hits the ramp at somewhere north of ninety miles an hour.

We're down the ramp, directly into the HOV lane, and on our way. This is the second time in recent weeks someone has driven an SUV like an insane person on my behalf. In Atlanta, this passes for normal.

Dez becomes calm as the eye of a hurricane, "We'll be there in fifteen minutes, which terminal?" she asks and adjusts her hair in the rearview mirror.

The airport is twenty-seven miles away.

"We won't get there at all if you don't slow down," BeeBee is upset.

She slows down, but not by much.

BeeBee, despite the obvious danger, unbuckles his seatbelt again and turns around to face me.

"You should climb back here with me," I suggest.

There's enough space, he manages the transition without much effort. He kicks Dez a time or two, which may not have been on accident.

He buckles in, turns to me and says "Spill it."

Which I proceeded to do, as quickly as possible. This takes

over ten minutes. I leave a few details out. He and Dez, for the first time ever, listen intently.

When I'm finished, BeeBee sits quietly for all of a millisecond and says, "Charlie, this is all bullshit."

"I know, bullshit. He's full…," I start, then BeeBee cuts me off.

"No, you don't know. It's your turn to shut up and listen, can you manage?" He asks, and I think he knows the answer. Those are two tall orders for me.

"I'll do my best."

BeeBee takes a pause, exhales, shakes his head, then starts to rock my world.

"Luke is not what he seems," he says, and I have to cut him off.

"He's not gay," I exclaim.

"You're not shutting up," BeeBee growls.

I make zipping motion across my lips.

"I thought something was fishy. I worked in the DA's office for a long time and never once met him. But his name was familiar to me; at first, I let it go. I was more focused on you than him."

I'm filled with a mix of guilt and pride and happiness and shame. It's like eating the best ice cream in the world, right before you find out you're lactose intolerant.

BeeBee continues, "He kept coming around the hospital, looking cute and worried, I thought he had a man-crush on you. Then he met us for lunch, and I swear he was flirting with Dez."

"Oh, he was," she says from the front seat, looking at us in the rearview, "he was most certainly flirting."

I want to interject with something along the lines of 'and you didn't think to tell me?' I decide it can wait.

"This bothered me, a lot. I decided to do an investigation of my own, but got sidetracked when Harvey came to me about you. He said you owed him ten grand and he needed the money to tide him over until you got yourself sorted out. You were in the hospital, he said it was urgent…"

I'm seeing those big picture dots again, and when I connect them, I'm drawing a different picture.

"I knew you guys had started a business together. I thought it was excessive, but he showed me the paper trail. He keeps records, you know."

Why no, I didn't know. Why does a drug kingpin keep records? Is it because he's a CPA, and not a drug kingpin? Could be. Anything is possible.

"I'm too busy with work, worrying about you, the non-profit, I don't know why, but I didn't dig too deep, I handed him an envelope of cash when I met him at the Majestic for lunch. He met me in the parking lot and asked for the money there."

Even I know what he's saying is weird. I say nothing.

"It should have been a red flag. He kept telling me how worried he was about you, and how much he appreciated the 'loan' until you could make things right."

"This is all my fault. BeeBee I'm sorry…," I start my heartfelt apology, but Dez isn't having it.

"Charlie, sweetheart, it's not your fault. Shut up and let him finish. Which terminal?"

"North, go to the lower drive up. L-one."

"After," BeeBee continues, "I felt like I had to prioritize Luke. I called some friends and they did some searching. The reason I knew Luke's name, I'd seen it before, probably dozens of times. You don't forget a name like Luke Goode, not for long." He pauses for a minute, to catch his breath, compose his thoughts, or for dramatic effect. Doesn't matter, it lasted long enough for me to want to break my silence.

He starts again, "Luke is not a cop, he's not a detective, he was an evidence tech for APD. He's also Harvey's brother-in-law, or was, before his divorce."

I feel my head exploding in slow motion. There's enough of a pause in the narrative for me to look at Dez in the rearview looking back at me and say, because I can think of nothing else to say, "He's bisexual."

And they both respond, at the same time, "I know."

"Their relationship is a tangled mess, too much to go into now," BeeBee says. He's about to say more, but we're approaching the terminal. Dez maneuvers through traffic, cutting around the slowly moving amateurs who have no idea how to get in and out of the airport.

"Let me guess," I say, before BeeBee can continue, "Luke got fired and now he wants some payback."

"It's more complicated than that," he responds, then shifts gears, "we can get into it later. What's your plan?"

"I'm still working it out. The first step is to get my suitcase, it's got all the evidence. It's the center of Luke's attention, I need to get my hands on it."

Approaching the drop-off area, Dez says, "Charlie if you get yourself hurt again don't expect me to come visit you in the hospital. I don't have it in me."

"Thanks for the encouragement Dez, I'll keep it in mind."

Before I get out, I ask, "Wait, what's up with you two? What were you doing in my neck of the woods?"

They exchange a look before BeeBee answers, "We were meeting with my lawyer."

"You have a lawyer? But you are a lawyer." I'm lost.

"Yes, Charlie, lawyers have lawyers," Dez says, as if she's talking to a five-year-old, which is probably appropriate in the moment.

"Seems… incestuous, cannibalistic, redundant, help me with the words here BeeBee."

He doesn't respond. Instead, as Dez pulls the Suburban to a stop along the curb, "We're not waiting for you. Wherever you're going from here, you need to find your own way."

I'm hurt by this. A ride share from the airport is expensive, I know this from experience. BeeBee must see it in my face, he tells me, "We're not waiting for you, but we're here for you. Do whatever it is you need to do, then call me."

I get out of the vehicle, where I'm promptly assaulted by the smell I know all too well. Jet fumes, diesel, and cigarette smoke. Airports are disgusting. I shut the door as the window is going down.

BeeBee leans across the seat and says, "We'll figure things out together. I have some calls to make. I might have some reinforcements to call in."

Dez takes off like a rocket and they disappear around the bend and into the never-ending flow of departing traffic.

I've never felt so alone.

Or determined.

CHAPTER TWELVE

My Bags

This might be a good time to fill in a few gaps. At least, this is my thought process as I'm standing there at the curb, wondering if going forward without a plan is such a good idea.

Gaps. If Luke isn't cop, how was he working in an evidence room? It must be some kind of civil service job. Or maybe he was a cop, until he got fired. I'll have to check this on the interwebs later, but it would make sense. Okay, consider that gap filled, for now.

I need to get moving. I make my way inside, down a stench-filled corridor. It smells like it was cleaned last decade. Then on a short escalator ride with a female voice imploring me to hold the hand rail, which I refuse to do. Talk about gross.

Another gap, if Luke had access to the evidence from Harvey's arrest, was the bag of joints truly light, or did Luke tamper with the weight? Major implications here. This gap stays open.

And what about Luke's kid? If he really has a son, and that son is Harvey's nephew, what does that mean? Maybe it doesn't mean anything, but there's something there that keeps tickling my brain. Another gap remains unfilled.

At the top of the escalator, I decide to stop thinking about gaps. One is enough for the moment. I hook a left turn into baggage claim and cut straight across toward the huge breezeway where arriving passengers come up a set of absurdly long escalators in waves of unwashed humanity, while relatives and drivers of limos await them with handmade cardboard signs. It might be the faster way, but I don't want to risk touching anyone.

I turn away from the streaming mass of flesh and pass through a hallway which takes me toward the main atrium. If you ever need it, this hallway is where the cleanest bathrooms in the airport are located. Trust me on this, I've been flying in and out of this airport my entire life. Some things you figure out because you need to, not because you want to.

I take a right and cut through the main atrium proper. There's a restaurant there currently called the Atlanta Chophouse and Brewery. It changes all the time. The brewery part gets me. Who brews beer at an airport? Precisely no one. It's my favorite place at the airport to get a steak and a few martinis.

Not today folks.

I pass the Chophouse and I'm in the south terminal. I bang another right to head towards baggage claim. As expected, this section of corridor is empty. I'm not far from baggage claim, I can see it ahead of me, when it dawns on me, I have no idea where I'm going.

Where do they take unclaimed bags? There must be an office, or kiosk, or something. I stop and think. This thinking brings up one more recollection about the airport. At the end of the north terminal baggage claim area, there's an Atlanta Police Department Precinct office. I may not be going back the way I came.

I step to a railing separating baggage claim from the pedestrian way I'm in, and look, first at the near end, then the far end. Closest to me there's a row of once-upon-a-time telephone cubicles in the process of being dismantled and removed. At the far end, there's a huge gaggle of luggage against a wall and a sign over a glass door, "Baggage Services."

Jackpot.

I make my way past the carousels disgorging the usual load of bags, suitcases, barely held together boxes, and all the other crap people pay money to check. I mean, I don't pay, but a lot of people do, judging by the money the airlines make off baggage fees. As I'm approaching the Baggage Services office, which henceforth shall be called the BS Office, I take a gander at the accumulation of lost possessions and, to my complete amazement, I see my bag, sitting there, waiting for papa to come and take it home.

Unfortunately, it's in cordoned-off area.

I can't walk up and grab it without being obvious. I would look like a thief and my luck, even though there's probably not a soul alive who would pay attention to someone grabbing a bag from this pile, I would get snagged as a luggage thief. I could try to talk my way through it, given I have the claim ticket.

Do I have the claim ticket?

I pull out my wallet, I see the square of paper in the I'm-gonna-put-up-a-fight slot, and as I'm trying to drag the bastard out, I lose my grip and send my wallet flying. It lands inside the aforementioned cordoned-off area. When I say cordoned-off, I could as easily say 'roped off' but it wouldn't be accurate. Accurate would be 'strapped off,' but it sounds dirty.

It's a bunch of those posts with black straps rolled up

inside cylinders on top of each post. When they want to create the illusion of a separate space, they pull the strap from one post and attach it to another, daisy-chain style.

I bend over, lean under the strap, and retrieve my wallet. When I turn toward the BS Office I step into the chest of an exceptionally tall and broad-shouldered woman wearing a tight, form-fitting uniform. She speaks first.

"I see you eyeballin' my bags. You don't need to be eyeballin' my bags. If you got ideas about takin' one of my bags, you got another thing comin'."

"No ma'am, no, I have a claim ticket for one of those bags. One of those bags is my bags, I mean bag," I say, trying not to look at her breasts. They're at eye level, and they're fantastic, avoiding them is impossible.

She's tall, muscular without being masculine, and as beautiful as the day is long. Think Grace Jones with a lot more flesh on her bones. Her hair is up-do perfection and she's got iridescent blue talons for fingernails. Again, not my thing, but I can appreciate a mountain without ever wanting to climb it.

"My face is up here," she says, pointing a talon toward her face to make sure I know where it is.

I crane my neck up and say, "I'm sorry, I'm in a hurry and, I'm sorry. I need to get my suitcase and get on my way. Sorry."

A new record for me, by the way. Most number of 'sorries' in a single conversation.

"You say you've got a ticket young man?" She asks, not without a healthy dose of intimidation. I seriously doubt I'm younger than her, but who am I to argue?

"Um, yes, yes, I, I'm trying to get it out of my wallet. It's puttin' up a fight and I'm losin'."

"Mmm, hmm, let me see it," and by 'it,' she means my wallet.

I hand over my wallet and, with nails like long sparkling blue swords, she rips the ticket out quicker than taking money from an ATM. In other words, easy.

"I need this too," she says and takes out my driver's license, gives it good look. "Follow me, Mister Barnes."

I do as I'm told and follow her into what I immediately recognize as her personal domain. Pictures of her, some kids, her mother or her grandmother and who knows who else, all over the desk behind the counter. She's got a TV, a radio, a mini-fridge, a microwave. It's like one of those tiny houses millennials are keen on living in, but she's not a millennial. Or tiny. Judging by this, and the volume of unclaimed bags, she doesn't get many visitors. Something also tells me when she does, they're not nice to her.

She steps behind the counter, using her hip to shove a chair out of her way. I think this is a well-rehearsed move because the chair spins around and parks itself at the desk without making contact with anything else in the room. Amazing.

She taps away on a computer keyboard with her long blue, curved-and-pointy nails, staring at a monochromatic screen. Her equipment is ancient, but she gets results in a hurry.

"What con are you runnin' with me Mister Barnes?"

"It's Charlie, you can call me Charlie. What do you mean?"

"I'm about to call the police, Mister Barnes, if you don't fess up. And you can call me Mizz Jamie, we're not on a first name basis. This bag was claimed already. I'm asking you again, what are up to?"

"No, nothing, it's a mistake. My bag is out there, I can see it. I know it's there. Check it, I can go get it and show you." I'm feeling desperate, a fight or flight instinct kicks in. I turn to get the suitcase and her voice stops me in my tracks.

Slowly, with intensity, she says to my back, "Don't you take one more step towards my bags Mister Barnes."

At this point I'm wondering if she has a gun. She's wearing

a uniform, but I didn't notice a gun. But I'm not the observant type. Let's assume she has a gun. I raise my hands and don't turn around. I'm about to plead my case for my case when she says, "Put your damn hands down Mister Barnes. Turn around and talk to me."

"Mizz Jamie," I start, as I slowly turn around while lowering my hands, "I am not trying to insult you or steal from you. I need to get my suitcase and I'll be on my way. Would you mind checking the ticket against the brown roller-bag with the rainbow flag name tag and the big orange stripe around the middle, please? It's at the end of the first row of bags."

She thinks about it for a hot second, then says, "Please take a seat, Mister Barnes, back here," with an emphasis on the 'here.'

Fight or flight is becoming 'get the hell outta here.' I resist the feeling, shimmy around her, and sit at her desk.

"Do not move and do not touch," she commands, pointing her index talon at me like a weapon. She leaves me there alone and I ponder her amazing nails and wonder how much they cost. Yes, my mind goes there. I might want some like hers one day, for fun, and possibly self-protection.

In the short time she's out of the office I look over her family photos. I land on one, of her and three young men and one older. The family, I presume. No wonder she's tough. Anyone who raises three sons knows a thing or two about wrangling men.

She comes back with the bag, carrying it, not rolling it, which I take note of but don't fully appreciate in the moment.

"Something's not right," she says, confused, and less intense. Her attitude alleviates some of my fear, of her, but raises new concerns.

"This bag," she continues, "was logged in the system a while ago, then its status changed to missing, and here it is again. This isn't right, Mister Barnes."

"I don't know what to tell you. I've been in the hospital, recovering from an accident."

While I'd been waiting for her, I assumed the situation was a computer glitch or mis-entered number or some such problem. Looking at her standing in the door of the BS Office, while I'm seated at her desk, I come to the conclusion Mizz Jamie takes her job seriously. She cares about 'her bags.' She has a mystery on her hands. I have nothing to offer her by way of help in solving it.

But this does get me thinking. What if it's not a mistake? What if someone surreptitiously picked it up, then surreptitiously returned it. I've always wanted to use 'surreptitiously' in a sentence, this is a first for me and I got do to do it twice. Wait. Three times! I'm amazing.

But why? And how?

"Mizz Jamie, I see you run a tight ship here, but your computer is ancient, could it have a glitch?" It's a stretch but I gotta try something.

She considers this carefully, then says, "Come on around here Mister Barnes, I need to check something out."

This does not feel good.

She backs out of the minuscule office to let me get in front of the counter, then steps back in and starts beating the living daylights out of her keyboard. I expect keys to come flying off at any moment, or sparks. I get the sense she's looking for anything to offer up an explanation, to put this to rest and move on with her day, whatever her day looks like.

"I got it. Looky here," she says and beckons me back to her side of the counter.

I lean in as she points at a screen full of incomprehensible gibberish and says, "I got a bag here with no ticket, got logged before I got to the office. I'm bettin' they crossed up my records. The after-hours crew is always a temp or somebody they pulled from some other job, they don't know how to use my system."

"I'm sorry to hear it Mizz Jamie," and I mean it. I think I like her. I want her to be successful. But something tells me she's grabbing at straws on this one.

"You don't have to apologize Mister Barnes. You've been patient with me. I apologize to you for holdin' you up. Step back around there and I'll get you taken care of."

I'm exiled from Mizz Jamie's world once again, and I feel the relationship shifting. It's sad for me, I don't know why. I thought we were connecting.

She taps away at her keyboard with diminished intensity, then looks up and says, "Okay Mister Barnes, you're ready to go. I do apologize once again for the delay."

She hands over my wallet and driver's license. Time for charm. "Mizz Jamie, there's no need to apologize to me. You're a real pro, you care about your job. You've done me a solid, you sorted this out in no time at all. I appreciate it."

I reach out my hand, she smiles and takes it without stabbing me, gives me one single hardy handshake, and says, "Thank you, Mister Barnes, you have a nice day. And if you lose your bag again, I'll be here for you."

"Same to you Mizz Jamie, you have the best day you can have." I don't know why this slice of life has me feeling good. It's like the feeling right after your coffee kicks in on a sunny Saturday morning and everything feels awesome. I turn to leave and as I begin to roll my suitcase toward the door, all those good feelings vanish. My suitcase, the one packed full of illicit goods, is impossibly light. I don't have to lift it to know, even with wheels it should have some resistance to movement.

The suitcase is empty.

***

* * *

I resist the urge to drop to the floor and open the suitcase then and there. I head toward ground transportation, then change my mind and head toward MARTA. Today, MARTA goes somewhere I want to go. For a few bucks, it will practically take me to my front door. Yes, it can take me from my place to the airport too. Technically, it has always gone somewhere I want to go. But I would rather be driven when I want to fly.

Aside from the need to get home, MARTA makes sense today. MARTA will allow me to get home unnoticed. If Dumb-Dumb Gerry is there, parked on the street, I'll deal with it when I get there. It's a good plan, I like it. I like the fifty bucks I don't have to spend on a ride share too.

I roll my light-as-a-feather suitcase along with me and notice a woman and teenage boy looking at me, leaning in to talk to each other, then finally she points at me as I'm walking by and shouts, "Charlie Barnes, you're Charlie Barnes, aren't you?"

Are you kidding me? I have a fan. Wait, this didn't go well last time…

Normally, my ego would require me to stop and get a good stroking, but today I want to keep moving. Until the teenager, apparently her son, says, "I liked your book Mister Barnes."

I stop. He's too young to read my books. What is wrong with parents these days?

"Which one?" I ask, because if he says the second one, I'll know he's full of shit and I'll get on with my business.

"Captain Butch and the Space Pirates of Enkidu, is there another one? Did you write a sequel?"

"No way, nobody liked Captain Butch," I say and I'm about to walk away when I hear the mom say, "Ask him, go on."

"Ask me what?"

The kid reaches into a backpack, because all kids at all

airports everywhere in the world have backpacks, and pulls out a well-worn hardcover of my second book. He holds it up to me like Oliver with an empty gruel bowl and asks, with the sincerity that tells me his soul has yet to be ruined by the world, "Would you sign it for me, please?"

I look at him, I look at the mom, then I ask her, "Is he old enough to read my books?"

"He's mature for his age. I read it first. It's ok with me since it didn't have any graphic sex. The language is a bit much, but nothing worse than he hears at school."

I look back at him and take the book, "I don't have a pen."

This gives the mom a chance to say, "We were sorry to hear about your troubles. Are you doin' okay?"

"They tell me I'll survive."

"I'm glad to hear it, Mister Barnes," she says. "Your nose looks almost healed, you can hardly tell it was broken, it's practically straight."

It takes me a few seconds to think of something to say. Plenty of obscenities come to mind. I embrace the Leave it to Beaver moment with, "Gee whiz, thanks."

The kid has fished a pen out of his bag and is aiming it at me. I take it from him and ask "Why did you read my book? It's not exactly young adult." He's a clean-cut kid, maybe fourteen, with a boy-next-door demeanor. Everything about him says best little boy in the world, from his white Adidas sneakers to his short sleeve button down and crew-cut hair.

He blushes, looks down at his feet, then looks back at me and lowers the boom.

"I like science fiction, but there's not a lot with gay characters, and when there is, it's usually like, full of sex or the character ends up dead, or they go crazy, or they're evil. Your book is full of gay characters, I mean, like all of them are gay. And nobody dies, everybody is happy and they're, like, people. Being gay just makes it more fun. I can see myself in the story. It's a weird story, but the people are cool."

"And there's no graphic sex," says his mom.

"Do you read everything before you let him read it?"

"Everything," she says and at the same time he says, "Not everything."

I have to laugh, as do they, and I imagine how well versed she must be in the tropes of gay erotica.

"What's your name?"

"Andrew."

"Do people call you Andy?"

"No sir. Well, there was this one kid who used to bully me all the time. He called me Andy, to tease me."

"And what did you do about this one kid?" I ask, because this is important to me. I might have to give him some Big Gay Uncle advice.

"Well, my mom told me you can't reason with a bully, you have to speak to them in their language. She got me Karate lessons. One day he wanted to beat me up. I smacked him a couple of times, then he started crying. He's pretty much left me alone ever since."

This kid is going places. I like him. I want one exactly like him. No, forget it, I'm too selfish to be a parent. "Pretty much?" I ask. This is fascinating to me. I've managed to forgot all about myself, and the heap of trouble I'm in, and focus on this one interaction. What's happening to me?

"Yeah, well, he stayed away for a while, then he came to my house with his dad. We're trying to be friends."

"Did you have to beat up his dad up too?"

Mom laughs at this and says, "Oh Mister Barnes, I do love your sense of humor."

Which I translate as 'stop asking my kid questions and sign the damn book.'

I look at the book in my hands and notice a page is dog-eared. I open to the page and read. It's an important chapter in the book, and this page in particular is critical. It's when Prince Reggie tells Captain Butch he loves him. It took two thirds of the book to get there, and it's the best writing in the novel. This kid has great taste. The most popular word used to describe my second book was 'juvenile.' Maybe this should be my target audience. I flip back to the title page and write what I hope is something meaningful.

For Andrew,
I hope you don't have to wait too long
to find your Prince Reggie.
Your mom is awesome, btw.
All the best,
Charlie

I hand back the pen and book, say, "It was nice meeting you both. Good luck to you Andrew."

Mom says, "Thank you," and Andrew says, "Can I get a selfie with you?"

It's not a selfie if I'm in it and your mom takes the picture, but okay. Besides, mom has the phone out, this should be quick.

"Sure, why not?"

I step next to him, put an arm around his shoulder in a way I hope is not creepy. He holds up the book, mom takes three or four shots, then it's over.

"Thank you, Mister Barnes, if you write a sequel I'll buy it," Andrew says, believably.

"I'll tell my publisher."

I turn away and resume my crappy life. Aside from making me feel good about myself at a time when I am not feeling good about anything, this interlude had a couple of important impacts.

First, it delayed me long enough that I didn't have to wait more than a few minutes for the train to arrive, once I made it to the platform. Second, when I turned toward the mom for the photo, I saw Harvey heading toward the BS office.

I'm pretty sure if they show the pictures to anyone, the first they'll ask is 'what's up with the look on his face?'

Because I definitely wasn't smiling.

***

Seeing Harvey at the airport makes me think about gaps again. It's a long ride on MARTA from the airport to my stop, about 90 minutes, on a good day. Dez covered the distance in less than twenty minutes, but hey, it's not a competition. On this day, the train is taking longer than usual. I have time to think, and I think about gaps.

I have no doubt Harvey is about to meet his match in Mizz Jamie, and I already have the suitcase, no worries here. But if Harvey is making a move on the suitcase, he must not know someone else already got to it, which definitely eliminates him as the culprit.

Which leaves Luke and Gerry the Pig Face.

Yes, I said I would stop with the names. I lied, sue me.

If someone grabbed the bag when the BS office was closed, assuming Mizz Jamie's un-ticketed bag error is a good marker, then it would have to be Gerry, or some as yet unknown player. This is getting me nowhere. I've got time to kill and the train is nearly empty. I decide to open the suitcase.

MARTA rail cars have a section for bike riders, an alcove at one end. Since most bike riders don't ride the train, this space is useless, unless you feel like standing up, or want to make out with your bestie and not be on full display.

Or you want to open a suitcase out of sight of the cameras at either end of the car.

I move to the alcove, lay the suitcase flat and unzip it. I pause before I open, I like the drama, then I flip over the top half. On this, I want to ask, how do you know which side is the top? I mean, isn't either side as likely to be the top? I say the top is whichever side happens to be facing up, and the one facing down is the bottom. It's not a fixed rule, it's about position.

BeeBee and I argued about this once. We got drunk one Cinco de Mayo in Cabo, it made perfect sense this would be a topic of conversation. I think I won.

The case is not empty.

There's a piece of paper. It's blank. I pick it up, turn it over, and in a flash some gaps are filled:

Screw you Harvey.

Pay up.

Not Luke. Not his handwriting. Gerry the Nut Sack got there first. He must have managed it while Luke was distracted having fun time with me. Harvey owes Gerry money. But why? Is it the ten grand Harvey gave me? Does it explain Harvey's insistence on giving a man-child like me ten thousand dollars? Desperation to pay back a bigger debt?

What does this mean for Luke? I'm supposed to be filling gaps, not making more. I toss the paper back into the case, zip it shut, and return to my seat to think. I'm lost in thought and barely notice when the train heads underground, signaling our approach to downtown Atlanta.

I don't tune back in until we hit Five Points, the biggest station in the system. Five Points, the part of the city by that name, not the station, is another one of those quirky but true, although not entirely true, things about Atlanta. Like Peachtree Street.

Five points gets its name from five intersecting streets, forming what some people view as the center of the city. For me, Midtown is the center of the universe, who cares about Five Points?

Someone chose to use the intersection as the starting point for the numbering of downtown streets, even though the converging streets don't line up with the downtown grid. This crap could drive me crazy if I thought about it too much, or I drove a lot. As a result, there is no first or second street in Atlanta. We start at three. Third Street. If you can find first street, running east-west, on a map of downtown Atlanta, I will give you a dollar. But remember, I lie.

I'm approaching my station, Midtown, four short stops north of Five Points. When I get there, I'm such a noob MARTA rider, I end up taking the wrong exit stairway and land on the north side of Tenth street. I get to stop traffic to cross the street mid-block. I will be hated. It's rush hour, which starts at three every weekday, earlier on Fridays, and ends around seven. Yes, our rush hour is four hours long, occasionally longer.

No one is going anywhere in a hurry, but drivers still get pissed when I stop traffic at the mid-block crosswalk, because people in Atlanta love to change lanes every two seconds, always trying to get one more car length ahead, like a road rage version of 'Frogger.'

If you don't know the game, take a break, Google it, find someplace to play it, then start reading again. I'll wait.

The interstate is even worse. People drive like they're all in some wide-open NASCAR race. It is the south, after all, we birthed the sport. It's insane when this happens in bumper-to-bumper traffic, millions of people jammed onto a highway moving at warp speed with barely a gnat's hair between them. It's perfect for Dez. I never drive on the interstate, the psychos can keep their craziness.

I cross the street, make my way to Crescent Avenue, and turn toward home. It's a short block, I can see my building at the end of it. There's a credit union on the right, at the end of Crescent, with the corner of the building sliced off to create a wide patch of street corner in front of the bank entrance. It gives me great visibility up my street before I reach the intersection, and gives me cover to look down the street.

I look down the street.

At this time of day, you'd expect the spaces to be mostly full, which they are. And as expected, there's a craptastic old Volvo parked in one of them. A part of me wants to walk down the street and get some payback. I start, then I see the car is empty.

A quick glance at my balcony catches sudden movement. I'm fairly certain I saw Gerry the Beast up there. Surprise, surprise. I stand there in the open on the corner like a fool for a few minutes, trying to figure out what to do next. I do what anyone in my position would do, I call BeeBee. I pull out my phone. Mine, not the trash one from the drugstore, and dial BeeBee.

"Where are you?" He asks, sounding stressed.

"My place," I reply.

Before I can say another word, he says, "We're heading up," and hangs up.

Either he's confused or we both are. I know I am. As I'm standing there, pondering whether or not I should call him back, I hear a voice from behind me which 24 hours ago made me feel warm and fuzzy. Now it sends a chill through my body.

"Hello handsome."

***

I have to think fast. Luke probably believes I still think he's up-and-up, which leaves explaining the suitcase. I manage a smile and turn around to face him.

"Luke," I say, trying to sound cheery, "I got the suitcase," and I lift it up to show it to him.

Not the smartest move.

"I see. Good boy Charlie," he says, thoroughly amused. "Shall we?" he asks, and motions toward the door of my building.

It's over. No more pretense. And he's got a gun. His windbreaker flapped opened and I saw it. I'm sure one day I'll get around to processing the fact this guy I've been falling for is standing in front of me with a handgun in a shoulder holster, under his flimsy navy-blue windbreaker. Where *does* he shop? I'm not gonna think about it. As they say, tomorrow's another day. If he knows someone is in my place, and he knows who, then one or more of them is in on his charade. Who else is in there?

"Have you been waiting long?" I ask, stalling. He's calm, it's worrisome.

"No." He nods his head at the door to my building again.

"It doesn't have to go down like this," I say, with what I think sounds like conviction.

Luke cocks his head to one side, like a dog listening to a strange noise, and says, "What way Charlie? What do you think is happening here?"

"You know what? Fuck it, let's get this over with."

"That's the spirit," he replies.

I surrender. I turn and start across the street, Luke close behind. How did I manage to completely screw myself? I'm glad Andrew-not-Andy isn't here to see this. We enter the building and climb the stairs in silence. I take my time, thinking this will give me time to think.

Luke isn't having it. He slaps me on my ass and says, "Giddy-up."

I'm embarrassed to admit I liked it. It's not my kink, far from it. But, you know, I liked it. And since I have the impulse control of a drunken monkey, I stop and tell him, "Keep it up and this will take all day." I know, this guy is not my friend. This guy is bad news. This guy is up to some bad business. I'm looking for a silver lining, something to make things less bad.

He finds it funny, reaches his hand out and lays it gently on my butt cheek, leans in and says, sweetly, "Pick up the pace Charlie, or the next thing I plant here will be my foot."

I can't help but visualize his foot in my ass, to conjure an indelible image of a truly disgusting idea. Then I move on, not much faster than before. As we ascend the stairs, passing the closed doors of my neighbors, I catch bits and pieces of their lives drifting out into the stairwell, a television tuned to the local news, the smell of something spicy cooking, a loud conversation. They're oblivious to my problems, and why shouldn't they be? It's not like I've tried to be friends.

Occasionally, I try to be a good neighbor, but it never lasts.

We get to the fourth-floor landing and my downstairs neighbor's door is open. I make note of the stacks of moving boxes and wonder if this is moving out day or moving in. Do I have a new neighbor? I hope I do. I'm sick of listening to the last one gripe about noise. My noise. Good riddance.

We step up to the last midway landing before switching back at the corner to take the final steps to my front door. I have a landing all my own, since the entire fifth floor is mine. Yes, I 'm bragging. It's pretty much all I've got, materially speaking, I might as well make something of it. We're about to arrive on the landing, and I hear shouting from inside. It sounds like BeeBee shouting obscenities at someone. We stop a few steps below the landing. What follows happens in seconds, or nanoseconds. Whatever, it happens fast.

The noise escalates rapidly, more than one voice, shouting. Glass breaks. Something wooden snaps. It sounds like a strung-out 70s rockbound is doing their trash-the-place version of extreme home makeover. Then we hear this loud thumping, like an elephant charging, coming toward us from the other side of the door.

I look at Luke and he steps behind me. I become a human shield. I assume he's about to draw his weapon. I look back at my front door in time to see it explode towards me. Anyone who's ever stepped through a front door knows they open in, not out. Doors are not supposed to open in this direction. Technically, it didn't open, it exploded outward, which leaves the laws of the universe intact. A tsunami of shattered wood is heading my way, followed by a large human body, followed by another large human body, attached to the chest of the first.

I reflexively turn away, towards Luke, pull the suitcase up to my chest, then cringe, after which the mass of splinters and bodies slams into my back.

Let's talk about Newton's Third Law of Motion, or as I like to call it, NTLM. I think it might be relevant and enlightening. In its simplest form, NTLM says for every action there is an equal and opposite reaction.

If, for example, you throw a ball and it hits something, the force of the ball is imparted to whatever it hits, with some degree of force being imparted back to the ball, usually slowing it down, if not fully stopping it. I learned this lesson well as a catcher. Imagine all the force it took to shatter my admittedly thin, partially cracked, although still solid, wooden front door. All of the force is being imparted to me. Aren't I lucky?

Two bodies, a bunch of wood, me, and finally my suitcase, all slam into Luke, with an extra kick from gravity, since our combined mass is going down a flight of stairs. A point worth noting here - Luke did not have his gun drawn. It's a minor holiday miracle.

The suitcase I'm holding at my chest is empty, it doesn't add much mass to the equation. What it adds is a spring action, with compression coming from a combination of the falling bodies and resistance generated by making contact with Luke. Did I mention my suitcase is hard-sided? Hard plastic all around. Luke is shot down the stairs like one of those circus performers being shot out of a cannon, sending him smashing into the large window opposite the stairs.

The window is a bunch of six inch by eight-inch panes of glass, all set in a wide steel lattice-work frame running the width of the landing. Hopelessly inefficient in the thermal sense, but nice to look at.

Luke hits it, hard.

Windows panes shatter, I hear a voice I assign to my new neighbor shout, "Holy shit, what the hell?" Luke slumps to the floor. He's toast. The amount of force imparted back to me by Luke's body, on first contact, is minimal, relative to all the force behind me. As it happens, I am lucky. The contact is enough to deflect me to one side, out of most of harm's way. Minor holiday miracle number two.

I fall on top of the suitcase, which implodes, as it should, according to NTLM, and the two bodies, who owe me a new front door, continue on, body surfing across my lower back, cruising on down the steps.

I impart some minimal force back to them, enough to keep them from careening all the way down to the next landing. Instead, they land, one atop the other, with a strange sound, a combination of a loud slap, a short pop, a low thud, and a sharp exhale of air. Like a boulder dropping onto an extremely large frog.

I am hurt, but I've had worse. My ribs scream at me, and a clutch of splinters make a new home in my back and side. My feet are aiming up the stairs, my head is aiming down, facing the outer wall of the stairwell. As I'm untangling myself from myself, I see a woman in a police uniform at the top of the stairs, with a look of shock and horror locked onto her face.

She says something into a radio attached to her shoulder, while at the same time, I hear a stampede of footsteps echoing up the stairwell toward me. I roll over to see the two bodies a few steps lower than me. Two men, one fat, the other athletic and absurdly tall.

BeeBee has used Frog-belly Gerry as a bouncy toy.

Gerry, like Luke, is toast. BeeBee, on the other hand, is looking back at me and smiling. His head and face are bleeding, and he's as upside down as me, laid out on top of a fat, unconscious, grotesque man, and he's smiling. Never, ever, question my love for him.

He laughs at me and yells, "Chaarrrrllliieeee, next time somebody wanna to put a hurt on me, bruh, you let me have 'em. I didn't grow up fancy like you, I can manage, you see?"

I have to laugh. I mean, what a hot mess. And I love it when he breaks out the accent.

I swing my feet around, stand, and help him up off The Mound Formerly Known as Gerry the Fake, and he hugs me with one of his death-grip hugs I will never grow tired of, and will miss more than a drunk misses booze if he ever stops.

A horde of Atlanta's Finest begins to arrive at the landing.

The female cop at the top of the stairs is still talking into her radio and more cops arrive behind her. The female cop calls down, "Mr. Barkin, are you injured?"

BeeBee releases me, returns to his, 'I'm large and in charge professional voice' and replies, "I think we're okay, Officer Park. Nice work."

The arriving cops are checking the condition of Luke and Gerry when my new neighbor, who probably was never told about the noisy jackass upstairs, steps through his door, takes in the scene, and looks up at me.

As should be abundantly clear, I am a dick. I have a hard time filtering myself, because I don't often try. If it's in my head, it will probably pass over my lips. "Welcome to the neighborhood," I say with a smile.

"Fuck me" he says, to himself. Then again, he's handsome. It might have been an invitation for later.

"Go upstairs Charlie, we have some things to talk about," BeeBee says, offering up the world's greatest understatement. He goes down the steps to the landing, weaving through the gathering police force and the two, apparently not dead, bodies. He stands in front of the newcomer to the building and starts with, "I'm sure you didn't expect this when you moved to the neighborhood, but trust me…"

The rest is lost to me after I turn, pick up my now flattened suitcase, and walk up the stairs.

The female cop, Officer Park, who I likely owe my life to in some way, says, "Welcome home Mr. Barnes."

She says this with a smile on her face. Because turnabout is fair play, and I've got no witty comeback, I simply say, "Thank you, Officer."

CHAPTER THIRTEEN

Spill It

All those gaps. All those dots. The truth about Harvey, Luke, BeeBee, me, my suitcase, the whole sordid, ridiculous, shameful, insane story finally makes sense. No more gaps. Most of the dots I tried to connect fall into place. The rest fade away as the full image resolves.

After the smash-up derby in my stairwell, BeeBee and a couple of detectives, along with a few cops, gather with me in my living room, Harvey was already there. The room is a wreck, as expected. We rearrange the furniture to accommodate everyone.

Harvey, I'm shocked to see, looks like he's at death's door. I hadn't paid his condition much attention. I had closed my mind to his appearance. He's sitting in my comfortable armchair and looks like he could fade into the fabric. I never wanted to acknowledge his impending death, but it's inescapable. I wonder again how he's kept all of this going.

One EMT took a few minutes to clean up BeeBee's face, while another took a look at my back, carefully extracting jagged pieces of my front door. During this time Harvey sat in silence, while the various members of law enforcement made small talk about food or sports or beer.

BeeBee eventually hands out fancy bottled water to everyone, then grabs a chair from my dining table. A woman wearing a pants suit in place of a uniform, Hilary Clinton-style but far less colorful, sits next to him. It doesn't take long to figure out she's the boss. She kicks off the conversation with, "For those who don't know me, I'm Captain Josette Butler. Here's how this is gonna go." She pauses to make sure everyone is paying attention.

"Mister Barnes, Mister Barkin has filled me in on your part in this circus act. The District Attorney will need a statement from you. It can wait until tomorrow, I'd like you at her office before noon. I suggest you bring your lawyer, think you can manage?" she finishes, and looks in BeeBee's direction.

I look at BeeBee and he nods back, I say, "Yes sir, uh ma'am, sorry."

She grins, I'm sure she's been called sir more than a few times. Doesn't faze her a bit, and why should it?

"Mister Wahl," she says to Harvey, "I'm well versed on your involvement in this scheme as well. You'll be a guest of mine tonight. Do you have an attorney?"

Harvey looks at BeeBee, who stares back like a lion ready to eat a rival's cub. Vicious. I love it. Harvey replies, "No."

"Alright then, we can help out there. Do you have someone you'd like to call?"

"Yes."

"Fine. You can make one call before these nice officers relieve you of your phone. Make it a good one." She makes a head movement to one of the officers standing by the front door, who walks over to Harvey.

Harvey struggles to stand, an officer helps him. Before he goes, he turns to BeeBee and says, "I'm sorry."

"I'm not your lawyer Harvey, but I advise you to stop talking."

Harvey turns to me, and I'm expecting the same apology. No dice. He doesn't want to open himself up to another rebuke, or he thinks I'm a bitch and this is all my fault, I don't care anymore. He nods his head at me as he walks by, heading out the door.

"Okay, two down, two to go." She turns to the EMT who treated BeeBee. "How are the meat sacks in the hallway doing?"

"On their way to Grady. The big one's stable. The little one is in worse shape but he'll pull through."

My mind wanders to thoughts of Luke laid up in the ICU. Will they treat him any different if he's handcuffed to his bed? Based on what I recall, they won't. I almost feel bad for envisioning him and the BMS getting to know each other. The feeling passes, quickly.

"Mister Barnes, do you have someplace you can stay tonight?" the captain asks.

BeeBee doesn't hesitate to say, "He'll be fine here. I'll stick around and help clean up the mess."

He's being sweet. He knows me. I'm not going anywhere tonight. Might as well quash the concept.

Captain Butler slaps her knees, stands up and says, "Great, good luck to you both. Don't forget tomorrow, before noon. Let's roll people."

As quickly as they arrived, they're gone. The shape of the stairwell amplifies the sounds of crunching glass and wood, as a small army marches through it. I'm sure my new neighbor is thrilled. When the sound dies away, I look at BeeBee and say, "Talk to me Goose, how bad is it? What's gonna happen to me tomorrow?"

BeeBee moves to the sofa, next to me, and looks at me with a sad, serious face.

Then the face melts into a smile, then laughter, then he gives my shoulder a shove and says, "Nothing's going to happen, you're gonna be all right."

"Seriously, BeeBee, what's going on?"

He continues to smile and says, "Charlie, don't worry. I've got it worked for you already." Then he begins to properly connect dots and fill gaps. "The current theory is Luke tampered with the evidence after my team began to review Harvey's case. There's a record of Luke visiting Harvey in jail a week before the evidence was weighed for the second time. Luke removed enough pot from the evidence bag to bring down the weight. Harvey gets out of jail, and has an actionable case against the city. When he won, he planned to share the proceeds with Luke. If he'd lost, it wouldn't matter."

"But Luke didn't count on getting fired."

"Probably not. And Harvey didn't count on getting cancer, or getting divorced, or having a kid with his mistress. All that not counting added up to a need for cash. Lots of cash. Harvey was under investigation already, you were a minor sideshow, but now you can bring the whole thing down."

"How's Gerry figure into all this?"

"Not sure, but I suspect he was more than the muscle, the captain thinks he's the ringleader. None of it was big time, but it was big enough. He's going away for a long time, this time."

"This time?"

"He was Harvey's cellmate for a while."

"I'm such an idiot, clueless. How is it I'm not in jail right now?"

"Because you have me to look after you."

***

The next morning the smell of coffee wakes me and for the briefest of moments I forget everything and think Luke is in my kitchen making me breakfast. Then it all comes crashing back, and the memory forces me out of bed and down the hall.

BeeBee is cooking up eggs and grits, a pot of coffee is brewing.

"BeeBee, what in God's name are you doing? It's…7:00 a.m., there's no reason…"

"A deal is a deal Charlie, and you got a good one. I'm not letting you screw it up. Good morning to you too."

"Why is everyone always expecting me to screw up?"

"You have to ask?" BeeBee says, placing his hand on my chest and turning me back toward the door, "Shave, shower, get dressed, you've got twenty minutes. March mister, that's an order."

BeeBee and I don't talk over breakfast, or during the short ride to the Fulton County Courthouse. We don't talk while we go through security. We don't talk when we're led to the DA's office. Yes, BeeBee knew the way, but he's a visitor this time, not an employee. We are led in silence.

We get to the DA's office and our handler says, "Miss Hollis, Misters Barkin and Barnes…"

She doesn't look up, keeps scribbling away on a notepad, points one end of the pen to her right, "I-3, I'll be there in a minute."

We're taken to a row of doors and number three is opened for us, "Have a seat, she'll be right along."

The room is plain, four chairs and a small table. There's a bizarro typewriter-looking machine on the table. The door shuts behind us and I feel the silence. It's complete, as in no noise from outside makes it into the room, and outside is noisy. I begin to speak, "BeeBee," and stop because it feels like I'm shouting. I drop my voice to a whisper, "BeeBee, what is this place? Why can't we sit in her office?"

"This is an interview room, and we aren't in her office because her office is not private, and she's prone to interruption. Relax, Charlie, this is normal."

"I don't like normal, never have. Normal is overrated."

He sits down and leans back in his chair. It's then I realize he's spent years in rooms like this. For Brian Barkin, it is normal.

"Normal is what you need. Sit."

He points at a chair and before I can stop myself I do as he says. Obedience is becoming habitual. I need a martini.

A young man wearing snazzy glasses enters, says, "Hi Brian" and sits down at the table.

"Hello Timothy, how you been?"

"Okay, place hasn't been the same since you left, but okay. You?"

It's a reunion, how cute. I wonder if they dated?

"Never a dull moment."

"I've heard. Mister Barnes, we're going to get started, Miss Hollis will join us soon. I'm going to ask you some basic housekeeping questions, then we'll move on to your statement, okay?"

"Do I have a choice?"

"Afraid not."

"Can I get something to drink?"

"Charlie," BeeBee says and stops. His look conveys the message.

"I'm ready, let's go."

He begins with things like, 'Spell your full name,' 'What is your current address,' 'How long have you lived there,' and blah and blah and blah. When the 'housekeeping' is over, on cue the DA enters the room, drops a folder on the table, sits down, opens the folder, looks at me and says, "Okay Mister Barnes, spill it."

And I do spill it. All of it. Five hours and multiple bottles of water, and the requisite bio-breaks later, I have told them everything. I do mean everything. The dress I wore on

Halloween, what Luke made me for dinner the first night out of the hospital, how many times Luke and I had sex, how BeeBee got mad at me and cried, how I got scared and cried, all of it, every single detail, including all about the drug mule stuff, the suitcase, you know, the boring parts too.

"And then we arrived here, straight from breakfast," is how I ended it.

DA Hollis, who by this time has been wringing her hands, tugging her hair, and generally being exasperated and miserable for five hours, looks at me, then at BeeBee. "Have you told us everything? You sure? You didn't mention what you had for breakfast this morning…"

"Eggs, over easy, grits, instant, two slices of toast, and a cup of coffee. I'm starving."

"Would you like something from the snack machine, a bag of chips, some Funyuns, a soda pop?"

"Yeah, I'd love it."

"No." She stands up, points at BeeBee, "Come with me please," then back at me, "you stay put."

They leave the room, it's me and Timothy. I've got no idea what's next.

Timothy's armpits are stained with sweat, he cracks his knuckles three or four times, then looks at me. He's about to say something, stops himself, then starts again. "I hope you appreciate what you've got, because from where I'm sitting, it doesn't look like you've earned it."

Before I can formulate a snarky comeback, he's gone, and the door makes a loud "click" when it closes. I try the handle and it doesn't budge. I'm a prisoner.

What felt like days, but was less than fifteen minutes, passes before Brian returns. I'm relieved to see him again, and thrilled he brought snacks.

He hands me a bottle of water and a sleeve of peanut butter crackers. "This should hold you over, it's going take a few minutes to print your statement."

"Print? Why can't they…"

"You have to sign it."

I know him well enough to know he's had enough of me for a while. It's a state of existence he manages to achieve from time to time. He's not mad at me, but he's given all the energy he can afford. It's like running on a treadmill. Sooner or later, you have to get off, but it doesn't mean you won't be back for more. The worst thing I could do in the situation is try to be funny. Good news is, I don't feel anywhere near funny.

"Brian," and he's surprised because he knows I use his real name when I want to be serious, "I need to ask you something. It's a big question, you don't have to answer it right away, but I want to ask. Do you mind?"

He shrugs, cocks his head to one side, then back to vertical, his body language for 'Whatever.' "Bring it," he says.

I lean closer to him and look directly into his eyes, "Why do you love me?"

He exhales, shakes his head, "Geez, Charlie, it's been a long day man…"

"I said you didn't have to answer right away."

"I'll answer your question, but it's the wrong question. You should be asking why I'm loyal to you."

"I like my question better."

"Charlie, listen, love, I don't know how to explain love. I don't know how to explain friendship, those are things, when they happen, you hold onto them as long as you can. Before I met you, I thought friendship was a word you used to describe someone who hadn't betrayed you yet. And love, I didn't think it was possible to love someone unconditionally. My mother told me, when she met you, she could see right into your heart, and all the stuff on your outside was there to cover up pain, or the absence of something you needed but didn't know how to get, but you behaved like you were part of our family and she loved it. She said she got the impression you didn't let your guard down unless you were around me. She said the same about me. She had some strange ideas about the world, but she knew people. She believed we were meant for each other, as friends, forever, the stars lined up for us, we were meant to be family. The why of it, does it matter?"

I didn't know if I wanted to jump for joy or cry a river. I did neither. "I'll need some time to process. How about the other question? Why are you loyal to me?"

"Because you're my friend. And because you were there for me, when I wanted to quit school and go back home…"

"I didn't know…"

"You changed my mind, all you did was make me laugh, you cooked me dinner on your shitty stove in your shitty apartment, we got drunk…you remember."

"Yeah."

"When my mother passed, you did the exact opposite. You told me you were there for me, whatever I needed. I needed to cry, you gave me the space to cry, to mourn. Charlie, you have been there for every important moment of my life since the day we met. You have had my back, like you had my back through all this," he points to the ceiling and spins his finger around in a circle, "and I know you'll always have my back, in ways no one else ever could. I'm loyal to you, you pain the ass, because you're loyal to me. I love you, you nut job, because you love me. That's it, that's all that matters."

I wanted to hug him but our moment was interrupted when the door opened and DA Hollis returned with a thick stack of paper. She dropped it on the table with a thud, slapped a pen down on top of it, pointed at me, then the stack, "Sign it, and we can call it a day."

I moved to the chair next to the table and read the top

page, a simple document by which my signature would attest to the truth of every word in the attached document. A document a couple hundred pages in length, despite detailing no more than two weeks of my life.

I signed it.

Then I looked up at DA Hollis and asked a question with the potential to alter the course of my miserable life.

"Can I get a copy of this, please?"

CHAPTER FOURTEEN

Aftermath

I often wonder what would have happened if BeeBee hadn't intervened at my place. Which, for the record, was a masterpiece of timing. BeeBee was heading to my place to fill me in on the deal of the century. He arrived moments before Luke approached me on the corner. He'd already contacted his friends back at the DA's office, who in turn call out the APD. There wasn't much time for planning, we got lucky. I got lucky.

BeeBee was parked behind my building, on the phone with me, when a single patrol car arrived, driven by the lovely, well-armed, and highly trained Officer Park. They entered the courtyard together and BeeBee saw me and Luke across the street. BeeBee insisted he and Officer Park had to get upstairs first, unaware there was already a party going on. Up the fire escape they went, running like the wind, with BeeBee taking the the stairs three at a time.

BeeBee, followed shortly after by the Officer, entered through the back door, made their way down the hall, and the confrontation with Gerry the Fetid Meatball ensued. You know how that turned out. Officer Park called for backup and the APD showed up in force, right after the whole thing was pretty much settled.

By the way, Gerry-Who-Looks-Like-Tweedledum pulled through. He may wish he died after he goes to prison again, but we'll see. Some people thrive in a highly structured environment. They struck the mother lode with him. In addition to the contents of my suitcase, they discovered a meth lab in his basement. He's got some interesting times ahead for sure. By the time all of the evidence was compiled and ready to present at trial, then paired with my sworn statement, the outcome was a forgone conclusion.

Gerry the Gorgon and Luke the Manipulator both made deals.

Otto von Bismarck once said 'God has a special providence for fools, drunkards, and the United States of America.' Since I'm two of those things, and associated with the third, I'm allowed to say he was right. I wish I were the exception proving the rule, but I'm not. Instead, I make the case for Mr. Bismarck.

Sadly, Harvey, may he rest in peace, died before Christmas. I think he gave up. Harvey had a multitude of opportunities to end, or avoid, the whole drama. He made bad choices, as did I, and a lot of people paid the price.

Anyone who thinks life is fair should think again. Life is not fair. It never has been, and never will be. Deal with it, and get over yourself. Expect to fight for everything, and frequently lose, and you'll never be disappointed. As for me, when news about my involvement in the traveling circus broke, I received the public humiliation I deserved.

I'm exaggerating. People hardly took notice once news of a unknown, rapidly spreading virus popped to the top of the news cycle. I didn't see why they cared, it was in China. We're not in China, my story should be more important. Then again, my story was beyond convoluted. Local reporters couldn't get it right to save their own lives. It wasn't fake news, it was a lack of research and a rush to get the story out first, or find their own special angle on it. Dez told me to keep quiet and ride the storm out, which I, being the new me, managed to do.

There was one incident, in Piedmont Park. I thought I was getting along famously with this handsome thirty-something who turned out to be a reporter for a newspaper in a neighboring state. Let's say it was Alabama, because, screw Alabama. We spent a couple of fun evenings together before he started poking around my story. He managed to get a little out of me before I caught on, but it was just the tip of the iceberg. Not enough for him to risk the scandal of using sex to get a story. Lesson learned for both of us.

Dez thought it was funny, and BeeBee, even now, thinks I should keep seeing the reporter. The guy's handsome, sure, but I don't need to replace one manipulator with another.

The best part, Dez didn't drop me. Because I didn't miss her deadline. I used the copy of my statement as an outline, made a ton of clever additions and edits, and voila, my book was finished. A draft anyway, we still have some work to do.

When I handed over my manuscript, I thought Dez was gonna cry. When she called me the next day to tell me she liked it, and it was my best work yet, I thought I was going to cry too. Of course, I've written three books, it's relative, take it for what it's worth. I didn't cry. She told me she laughed out loud at parts of it, and she cried at some, but overall, it was solid work. She didn't mention the hospital incident.

Finally, after I was silent long enough, and the media ran itself in circles trying to sort it all out, it was time. We already had a commitment with Andy Hooper over at CNN, which we delayed until the legal case was mostly wrapped up. It went about as well as you might expect. I don't think he likes being called Andy. But I insisted. Andy, Andy, Andy. I'm officially a bully.

All he wanted to talk about was the criminal case, my involvement, my time as a drug mule, all the ugly crap. I wanted to talk about my new book. I was a broken record, "It's in the book."

They're two similar topics, after all. It's a matter of the approach. He wanted to be a good journalist and I wanted to use him to build buzz before the book release. If he'd played along, we both could have benefited. Oh well, too bad for you Andy.

Pre-orders are killin' it.

During all the quiet time, I wrote. I had lots of material in my journal. You know all those happy factoids? In my journal, where they belong. It kept my mind off the insanity outside my four walls, and it is, after all, what I'm supposed to be doing with my time. If my life stays as interesting as the last few months, my next book won't take as long to write. I'll start publishing my journal entries every twelve weeks. Easy.

The day of my interview with Andy wiped me out. They wanted me to be there in person, and I obliged. The people were nice as can be, and not a fake southern nice. They practically held my hand through the entire process. When it was over, they gave me a coffee mug and showed me to the door. I was expecting a car to take me home, since one had brought me to the studio. Nope.

MARTA again, then up my five flights of stairs. Inside I made a beeline for the liquor cabinet. Martini o'clock had arrived. Before I could even open the cabinet, I heard a knock on my door.

In case you're wondering, my new door is steel. Looks old, has a grain in it like wood, but steel. I don't cut corners when it comes to home improvement, not anymore. It was BeeBee's doing, but so what, who cares. It's a damn strong door.

Knocking. On my new door. Probably a neighbor coming

to complain about something, because there's always something to complain about when you have shared walls and floors and ceilings. The new me doesn't ignore it, or yell 'go the hell away.' I opened the door. And I'm glad I did.

Standing there, handsome as the day is long, was my still relatively new downstairs neighbor. I almost didn't recognize him. I had no idea what his name was.

"Hi there." I think I sounded cheery. Maybe.

Downstairs Neighbor breaks out a huge smile and says, "Hi Charlie, I'm Eric. We met a while back." He motioned with his head, rather than pointing, because he was holding a plate of something covered in aluminum foil.

"Oh yeah, about that…"

"You don't have to say anything Charlie, water under the bridge."

"Sorry," and this was one of those rare occasions when I meant it.

"Don't worry about," he replied. "I know things have been pretty wild for you lately. I… I made you chocolate-chip cookies, Happy Holidays!" he rushed through this last bit as he thrust the plate toward me.

I wondered if this was BeeBee setup. How did he know chocolate chip cookies were my favorite? Nah, BeeBee didn't do this. Everybody loves chocolate chip cookies.

"That is awesome," I practically shouted, "you know what goes great with chocolate chip cookies?"

"Milk?" He took a stab, missed by a mile.

"Martinis. Wanna join me?"

He paused for a second, really gave it some thought. "Yes," he said, "I'd like that. I'd like that very much."

That's how Eric entered my life, cookies and booze.

But that's a story for another day, and it's a doozy.

Happy Holidays, indeed.

The End

Oh, wait, no, hold up. Almost forgot. BeeBee started dating a pilot, they're a super-cute couple. I'm already working him for free flights. Can't wait to tell you all about it. Okay, for real this time, The End.

About the Author

C.R. "Charlie" Barnes studied literature and journalism in college and went to work for a global news organization immediately after graduation. He now spends his time writing fiction because the news was never good, and one thing Charlie likes is a good time. "Happy Holidays!" is his first foray into LGBTQ fiction and its follow-up, "Adulting" might one day be written (if he stops slacking and starts writing again). He might change that title. We'll see. Visit beachbookpress.com to learn more.

Don't miss out!

Visit the website below and you can sign up to receive emails whenever C.R. Barnes publishes a new book. There's no charge and no obligation and we promise not to fill your inbox with junk. Plus, you'll have opportunities for discounts and giveaways - how fun is that?

https://beachbookpress.com/subscribe/

9 781965 621080